There he was: the infamous Will Ryan.

Pathetically, her palms felt clammy. Though that could just be the horrible cold she'd picked up on her way to California, she supposed...

But, truthfully, Cassidy Malone couldn't remember the last time she'd felt so nervous or so self-conscious. Or so completely incapable of fooling people into thinking she was more self-confident than she actually was. She really needed the latter if she was going to stand a chance of working with Will. And if she couldn't do it in the land of make-believe, then where could she?

Do you ever wish you could
step into someone else's shoes?

IN HER SHOES...

Modern-day Cinderellas get their grooms!

Now you can with Mills & Boon® Romance's
new mini-series brimming full of
contemporary, feel-good stories.

Our modern-day Cinderellas swap glass slippers
for a stylish stiletto!

So follow each footstep through makeover to marriage,
rags to riches, as these women
fulfil their hopes and dreams...

**This month step into Cassidy's shoes
to find out if this L.A. Cinderella
meets a movie-star-gorgeous prince in:**

**HIS L.A. CINDERELLA
by
TRISH WYLIE**

HIS
L.A. CINDERELLA

BY
TRISH WYLIE

MILLS & BOON
Pure reading pleasure™

First published in Great Britain 2009
Harlequin Mills & Boon Limited,
Eton House, 18-24 Paradise Road, Richmond, Surrey TW9 1SR

© Trish Wylie 2009

ISBN: 978 0 263 20776 7

Set in Times Roman 10½ on 12¾ pt
07-0509-49135

Printed and bound in Great Britain
by CPI Antony Rowe, Chippenham, Wiltshire

Trish Wylie tried various careers before eventually fulfilling her dream of writing. Years spent working in the music industry, in promotions, and teaching little kids about ponies gave her plenty of opportunity to study life and the people around her. Which, in Trish's opinion, is a pretty good study course for writing! Living in Ireland, Trish balances her time between writing and horses. If you get to spend your days doing things you love, then she thinks that's not doing too badly. You can contact Trish at www.trishwylie.com

For my new friend Lisa from Warner Bros. Studios
for the behind the scenes tour.

CHAPTER ONE

THERE he was: the infamous Will Ryan.

Pathetically, her palms felt clammy. Though that could just have been the horrible cold she'd picked up on her way to California, she supposed...

But, truthfully, Cassidy Malone couldn't remember the last time she'd felt so nervous or self-conscious. Or so completely incapable of fooling people into thinking she was more self-confident than she actually was. She really needed the latter if she was going to stand a chance of pulling off the deception of a lifetime. And if she couldn't do it in the land of make-believe, then where could she? If she just didn't have this stupid cold to add to everything else. Who flew halfway across the planet to a place twenty degrees warmer than home and ended up with a cold? She felt awful. So much for the theory that she would feel more confident away from home, where nobody knew her...

But therein lay her immediate problem. Because the man making his way across the beautiful lobby of the Beverly Wilshire knew her all too well. A decade ago he'd known every inch of her body intimately, and had held her heart in the palm of his large hand—the same heart that now jumped in joyous recognition and then twisted in regret at how comfortable *he* looked in their surroundings.

Cassidy was incredibly jealous of that.

Will didn't so much as bat an eyelid at the white marble, the large chandelier, the carved wooden elevator doors or the polished brass and black accents. *I belong here*, his confident stride said silently. But then Cassidy couldn't remember a time when there'd ever been a place he *hadn't* had that air of self-assurance. He'd always had a way of carrying himself that practically dared people to say he was somewhere he didn't belong.

That confidence, and the hint of potential danger if pushed, had added to his potent sexuality from the very beginning as far as Cassidy was concerned. Add boyish goodlooks and a smile that could genuinely melt female knees… He'd been the flame and she the moth. But to see him so at home in a place where she felt so very lost… Well, it just widened the already cavernous gap between them, didn't it?

Ridiculously, it hurt. When it really shouldn't have. Not after so long…

His bright green gaze sought her out and brushed nonchalantly from her head to her toes and back up again, forcing her to suck in her stomach and silently pray that he couldn't see any sign of the foundation underwear she'd struggled her way into. Like every woman Cassidy knew, every inch counted in times of crisis—even though she had absolutely no idea where those missing inches had been relocated *to*. With any luck Will would keep their meetings to places where there was air-conditioning, so she stood a better chance of not passing out in the California heat and the thin air of Los Angeles. Restricted circulation plus bunged-up nose didn't exactly give her a head start…

Mentally she crossed her fingers.

'Cass.'

He held out a ridiculously large hand when he got to her, and for a second Cassidy looked down at it with an arched brow, as if confused by what she was supposed to do with it. They were *shaking hands*? Like complete strangers? *Really?*

Okay, then.

Surreptitiously swiping a clammy palm on her hip, she placed it in his; the heat of long fingers curled around her cooler ones, sending another jolt of recognition through her veins to her heart. Good to know her body hadn't forgotten him either. She tried to think professional thoughts. It wasn't easy. But she had to *work* with this man.

Will let go of her hand somewhat abruptly. 'Recovered from your flight?'

'Yes. Thank you. I think it's easier this way than going back.'

'Happy with the hotel?'

'How could I not be?' She glanced around, but couldn't stop her gaze from shifting back to study him. Still boyish. He hadn't aged a day. How was that fair?

Will nodded, and glanced around him the way she had. 'It has a history firmly tied up in Hollywood. Dashiell Hammet wrote *The Thin Man* here. Elvis lived here while making movies at Paramount, and they've had everyone from members of the British royal family to the Dalai Lama stay at one time or another.'

'That's nice.' Inwardly she rolled her eyes as the words slipped off the tip of her tongue. Eloquent, Cassidy. Way to go. But, however foolish she felt, it was nothing in comparison to how stunned she was by his coolness. It was like talking to a tour guide. An uninvolved, unattached and in fairness disgustingly good-looking tour guide. But nevertheless…

'I thought you might appreciate it.'

Cassidy lifted a brow again. Meaning what? That she should be thanking her lucky stars she was here in the first place? True. But she didn't need to be made to feel as if she'd been invited to Tinsel Town by some miraculous accident. Some *timely* miraculous accident, she corrected. Because she couldn't have needed a break more if she'd tried.

He was right, though. She'd been as thrilled by the hotel as she had by her first glimpse of the Hollywood sign on the hill. Located only a few steps away from the glittering shops of Rodeo Drive, she knew the famous hotel's ornate European façade, with its distinctly rounded awnings and rows of sculpted trees, was straight out of the pages of Hollywood history—not to mention being the site of one of her favourite films of all time. It was just a shame she wasn't going to be there at Christmas, when they reportedly did an outstanding job of decorating, transforming its exterior into a dazzling display of twinkling lights.

By then she'd probably have been discovered as a fraud and sent home with her tail between her legs—back to eating rice and pasta like she had in her student days, while she'd waited for her grant money to arrive. Only this time she'd be waiting for meager pay-cheques that couldn't support the debts she had after caring for her father before he died. Well, now, *there* was something to look forward to.

'Ready?'

She nodded as Will swung a long arm in invitation and allowed her to step ahead of him. Squinting at the bright light outside, she took her sunglasses off the top of her head moments after Will donned his. A California necessity, she'd discovered since she'd landed. And as much of a status symbol as everything else, judging by the designer wear everyone but her had shading their eyes.

Silently, they turned right—Will matching his longer stride to hers—then right again at a major light, until they approached a strip of nice-looking semi-casual restaurants. Will's choice was an ivy-covered courtyard, where the *maître d'* greeted him by name and held out chairs for them before unfurling linen napkins onto their laps and handing them leather-bound menus with a flourish and a small bow.

Cassidy fought the need to giggle like a schoolgirl. At the grand old age of thirty, she should be more mature. 'Well, this beats cheese sandwiches in the park.'

Thick dark lashes flickered upwards from their study of the menu. They brushed his deeply tanned skin once, twice, and then he quirked his brows a minuscule amount and continued reading. 'That was a long time ago.'

Seeing him again, it felt like yesterday to her. But she didn't say that. Instead she allowed herself a moment to surreptitiously examine him while he made a decision on what to eat. Had he got sexier as he'd got older? Yes, she decided, he had. Darn it. Men were known to do that. Wasn't the fact he was more successful than her, richer than her and plainly more confident than her enough? At least one of them had got it right. Small consolation, though.

It was tough not to be as mesmerised by the sight of him as she had been at twenty. And twenty-one. And twenty-two. From the thick dark hair that curled disobediently outwards at his nape, all the way down the lean six foot three of his body, he was one of those guys blessed with the ability to mesmerise woman. Who could have blamed her for the crush she'd had from a distance for over a year? Or for how shy she'd been when he'd first talked to her during a group project in their screenwriting class? Or how…?

'Do you know what you want?' Will asked, in a low rumble that sent a sudden shiver up her spine.

The spine she straightened a little in her chair. Because, yes, actually—she did know what she wanted. She had a list, as it happened. High up on it was the ability to make the most of an opportunity when it came e-mailing her way, without blowing it by drooling all over the man who had long since left her behind. So now he'd given her an opening, it seemed as good a time as any to ask:

'A better idea of what the studio expects from me would be nice.' She even managed to tack on a smile when he looked at her again. See—she could do confident if she tried.

Will took a breath and closed the menu, calmly setting it down on his side-plate as he glanced around at the lunch-time crowd. 'They expect what they paid us that hefty advance for back in the day. We both knew what we were doing when we signed on the dotted line.'

Did *we?* If she'd known the heartache signing that contract would bring her way she wasn't so sure she would go back in time and sign it again. But Cassidy let it slide. 'So, after all this time they suddenly want script three? Just like that? When movie number two pretty much fell flat on its face…'

'At the box office. But thanks to a rabid internet fan base

it made money on long-term residuals. You'd know that from the fact we still get royalty cheques. This time we have the opportunity to be one of those sleepers that might well prove an accidental tent pole, with a good script and the right budget.'

Cassidy blinked at him for a moment, and then confessed, 'I have no idea what you just said.'

He almost smiled. 'Hollywood speak.'

'Is there a dictionary?'

'Not that I'm aware of.'

'Pity.' She tried another smile to see if it had any effect. 'You'll have to translate for me, then.'

'Bottom line?'

Oh, please, yes. 'That might help.'

Something resembling amusement glittered across his amazing eyes. 'They want a script yesterday, and as you and I own the rights jointly to the original copyright we've both got to do it. We're joined at the hip till it's done and they're happy…'

'No pressure, then.'

The wide shoulders beneath his expensive dark jacket lifted and fell in a brief nonchalant shrug. 'We did it before, Cass. We can do it again.'

The tiny word 'we' seemed to tug on a ragged corner of her heart every time he said it in his deep rumble of a voice. Not that it meant anything any more. He probably didn't feel the pressure she did. Why would he? He'd been writing scripts ever since he left—had success after success to his name: award nominations, contracts and his own production company. Whereas she, his former writing partner…?

Well, she had a knack for getting seven-year-olds to

stay quiet, but that was about it. The closest she'd got to writing was putting her lessons on a blackboard…

Automatically she reached for iced water the second a waiter poured it, swallowing a large gulp to dampen her dry mouth. A cold dew of perspiration broke out on her skin while she wondered when was a good time to confess how long it had been since she last written a single original word. Maybe just as well she hadn't unpacked properly yet.

The waiter smiled at her as if he felt her pain. So she smiled back.

Will's voice deepened. 'Have you done much writing?'

Oh, come on! How could he still read her mind when it had been so long since he'd seen her? It was the perfect opening for honesty; yes. But since she already had a shovel in her hand it seemed a shame not to use it.

'Not much scriptwriting. I've dabbled with other stuff.' In that she'd read instructional books—lots of them—to no avail. 'You know how it is. Use it or—'

'Lose it.' He nodded, the corners of his wide mouth tugging in a way that suggested he was fighting off one of the smiles that would addle her thoughts. 'This shouldn't take long, then. If you were rusty it might have taken a while to get you back up to speed.'

Cassidy swallowed more water to stop a confession from slipping free. Had it got warmer all of a sudden? She suddenly felt a little light-headed.

Out of nowhere he added, 'We made a good team once.'

She almost choked, her eyes watering a little as she looked at him and he finally let *that* smile loose. Oh, that was just unfair. She instantly hated him for it. With the white-hot intensity of a million burning suns she hated him for the fact *that* smile could still knock her on her ear. But even more than that she hated him because she'd been *waiting* for it to appear and knock her on her ear. She'd *known*! Had known from the second his name appeared in her In-box that he would have the capability to do damage to her self-control all over again.

But then being attracted to him had never been a problem. It had been his complete lack of availability to commit that had. She wasn't ending up the fool twice. She darn well *wasn't*!

Lifting her chin an inch, she set her glass safely on the white tablecloth and dampened her lips in preparation for saying the right words to make it plain to him it was strictly business between them this time round. After all, if she wanted to be made to look a fool she could do it all by herself. She didn't actually *need* any help.

But her resolve faltered in the sight of *that* smile. Light twinkled in his eyes, fine laughter lines fanned out from their edges, the grooves in his cheeks deepened, and his lips slid back over even teeth that looked even whiter than she remembered when contrasted with the golden hue of his Californian tan.

Put all those things together and it was infectious. Cassidy could even feel the reciprocal upward tug of her own mouth. No, no, *no*—she mustn't smile back. That was how it had started last time.

Will's deep voice added words husky with appreciation. 'You look beautiful—as always…'

The woman inside her so lacking in self-confidence blossomed under the simple, if unfounded praise. She

could feel her skin warming, could feel her heart racing—
could feel her smile breaking loose…

Then a sultry female voice sounded above her head. 'As
always flattery will get you everywhere, Irish boy…'

Whipping her head round, Cassidy found herself staring
up at a face she recognised from movie billboards and TV
screens. The woman wasn't just beautiful, she was perfection. Even without airbrushing.

When Will pushed his chair back, the actress stepped over
to him and kissed each of his cheeks, European-style. 'I
heard you got a green light for your pet project. Bravo, you!'

'You know what I had for breakfast this morning too?'

'Not in a long time.' She aimed a wink at Cassidy, who
smiled weakly in return. 'Not that you haven't been invited
often enough…'

Will remembered his manners. 'Angie—this is Cassidy
Malone. Cass, this is—'

'Angelique Warden. Yes, I know.' Cassidy made the smile
more genuine as she stood up and stretched a hand across
the table. 'It's nice to meet you. I loved your last movie.'

'Shame the box office didn't feel the same way. But
thank you.' Her eyes narrowed momentarily. 'Wait a second.
You're not Cassidy Malone as in *Ryan* and Malone?'

Cassidy's gaze slid briefly to Will and then back. 'A
long time ago…'

'Then the rumour is true? They picked up the option?'

Will nodded, and glanced around him as if it was a state
secret. He even lowered his voice. 'It's not been announced yet, so—'

'Oh, you don't have to tell me, you idiot. *How exciting!*'

Suddenly Cassidy was much more interesting to her than

before, and a matching set of European cheek kisses were bestowed on her before Cassidy could warn her of her cold.

'So nice to meet you. Make him bring you to dinner. I have a million and one questions to ask about the Ryan and Malone years. Will thinks being enigmatic makes him more interesting.'

'Not everyone likes their every move reported in the dailies.'

Still blinking in stunned amazement at having been kissed by one of the highest paid actresses on the globe, Cassidy found her attention caught by the drawl of Will's newfound American twang. The words made her scowl in recrimination. He'd been many things back in the day, but cruel had never been one of them. The famous Angelique Warden had hardly had an easy time with the press in the last year.

But Angelique laughed huskily and batted his upper arm with her designer purse, pouting and rolling her eyes. 'Yes, but it's such a joy for the rest of us. Dinner. Saturday. Bring your partner. I'm going to learn all your darkest secrets.'

'No, you're not.'

'I'll ply her with alcohol if I have to.' She winked at Cassidy for the second time and Cassidy was immediately charmed by her.

In fairness, if she plied the only Irish native on the planet who couldn't hold her drink with alcohol then she would get everything she'd probably never wanted to hear. Half a glass of wine and Cassidy's tongue tended to take on a life of its own.

'No, you won't. I need her lucid for the next few weeks.'

'Was he always so serious?'

Cassidy looked at Will, found him staring at her with a

disconcertingly unreadable expression, and her answer kind of popped out. 'No. He wasn't.'

He stared at her until she could feel her toes curling in her shoes.

So she bravely lifted her chin in challenge.

After what felt like a very long time, Angelique laughed musically. 'Okay, then. Well, you two kids have fun. I can highly recommend the scallops. Saturday, Irish boy—you hear me?'

'I hear you.'

He waved an arm to indicate Cassidy should sit back down, and she was glad of it. She really was starting to feel light-headed. Maybe she should have dragged herself out of bed for breakfast after all?

'I'll call on Saturday and tell her we can't make it.' He re-opened his menu. 'I think we should start brainstorming tomorrow and get something down on paper over the weekend.'

That fast? Great. Now she felt nauseous as well.

Hiding partially behind her auburn hair as she lowered her chin to scan the menu, she cleared her throat and asked, 'You have any ideas?'

'A few.'

It was like pulling teeth. 'Any you'd care to share?'

When she glanced at him she saw the slight upward pull on the corners of his mouth before he answered. 'Not here, no.'

Cassidy's gaze moved from side to side and she lowered her voice to a stage whisper. 'Are they watching?'

'They?' His gaze rose, curiosity lifting his brows.

'The script gremlins…'

There was a second of silence, and then a brief rumble of low laughter broke free. 'Haven't changed, have you?'

Oh, how little he knew.

They managed small talk after that. The latest movies Will's company had produced, the differences in living in California compared to Ireland… They even segued from there to the *weather*. But she couldn't help missing the ease they'd once had with each other. Angelique was right— Will *had* got serious with age. It made Cassidy feel like even more of an idiot. She couldn't seem to manage a conversation without a wisecrack or teasing him the way she'd used to, and it added to her feeling of awkwardness. Then she hit rock bottom in the embarrassment stakes when he walked her back to the hotel.

The air really was thinner in California. And it really was incredibly warm. Food hadn't got rid of her light-headedness. Her nose felt more blocked than ever, her throat hurt, and her voice was beginning to fade…

Then, back in the foyer of the beautiful hotel, surrounded by beautiful people in expensive clothes, Will turned to say goodbye and the world began to spin. The edges of her vision blurred—she swayed. And, as she had figuratively speaking so many years ago, Cassidy fell at his feet.

She came to with her head resting against Will's hard chest, his warmth surrounding her. He must have sat her up. He had his arm around her. Blinking the world into focus, her eyes immediately sought his.

He was frowning. 'What happened?'

'If I had to guess, I'd say I fell down,' she informed him dryly.

'Are you sick?'

'Bit of a cold. I spent the morning in bed.'

His mouth narrowed into a thin line as he held a glass of water to her lips. 'You should have said something.'

Allowing the water to wash the dryness from her mouth and throat, she glanced around at the sea of interested by-standers and immediately felt colour rising in her cheeks. Great. The never-ending humiliation continued. It reminded her of that time in high school, before she'd had laser surgery, when she'd forgotten her glasses and got into the wrong car outside the school gates. She'd held a five-minute conversation with a complete stranger before she'd realised what she'd done…

Irritation sounding in her voice, she tried to push up on to her feet. 'I'm good now, Will. Thanks. Let me up.'

But he held her in place. 'Give it a minute.'

When he held the glass back to her mouth, her sense of mortification was raised several notches. She pushed his hand away. 'Stop that. I can do it. I don't need a minute.'

Taking the glass from him, she struggled anything but gracefully to her feet, splashing water onto her hand and the floor. Once she was upright, she swayed precariously. Will stepped forward—one hand removing the glass, one arm circling her waist as he calmly informed her, 'That went well.'

Cassidy scowled at the grumbled words as he handed the glass to a hovering concierge before demanding, 'Key card.'

'What?'

'Give me your key card.' Lifting his free hand in front of her body, he waggled long fingers. 'Hand it over. You're going back to bed.'

'I don't think—'

'Good. Run with that. *Key card.*'

While her brain tried to think up an argument against the new and not necessarily improved attitude he seemed to have acquired with age, her traitorous hand reached into her bag for the card. Apparently the best she could come up with in reply was, 'I don't remember you being this bossy.'

'Comes with the territory in my job.' His fingers closed around the card.

'Can we get anything for the lady?'

Will nodded at the concierge's question. 'You could send up some chilled orange juice to room…?'

When he lifted his brows at Cassidy, she sighed. 'Ten-twenty-eight.'

'And send out to the nearest pharmacy for cold medicine of some kind.'

The concierge nodded. 'Of course, sir.'

Completely out of nowhere, Will did the last thing she'd expected and bent at the waist, scooping her into his arms like some kind of caped superhero. The man would put his back out! She was a good twenty pounds over the weight she'd been the last time he'd pulled that stunt.

A part of her curled up and died even as her arm automatically circled his neck. 'Put me down, Will. I can walk.'

As she whispered the words her gaze met that of several fascinated observers, and a couple of women who looked distinctly as if they were swooning. Now her cheeks were on fire. 'Will, I'm serious! I'm too heavy.'

'No, you're not. Shut up, Cass.'

She wriggled, and felt her lunch rearrange itself inside her stomach, drawing a low moan from her lips. If she threw up in public she was taking the next plane home. It would serve Will Ryan right if she threw up over *him!*

He walked through the remainder of the foyer as if she weighed nothing, and then turned to hit the elevator button with his elbow. Adding even further to her nightmare, he then moved the hand at her waist and dropped his chin to frown at her body. 'What *are* you wearing under that blouse?'

Oh. Dear. *God.*

'I think you'll find we're eight years too late for a conversation about my underwear.'

When he looked at her, she summoned a smirk.

His green gaze travelling over her face, he took in her flushed cheeks and the way she was chewing on her lower lip before he looked back into her eyes. 'Wearing something so tight that it restricts your breathing is hardly going to help any, is it?'

'It's not like I *planned* on falling at your feet.' Oh, she just didn't know when to stop, did she?

Amusement danced across his eyes. Before he could say anything the elevator doors opened, so he turned sideways and guided her inside. 'Push the button, Cass.'

She did. Then Will took a step back and lifted his chin to watch the numbers as they lit up above the doors.

'You can put me down now. Seriously.'

'That's not happening.'

Cassidy sighed heavily. His stubborn streak, she remembered. When Will had dug his heels in over something he'd been an immovable object. It had led to more than one heated debate when they were writing, but back then they'd had one heck of a good time making up afterwards. Naturally now she'd thought about *that* her body reacted.

So she tried to think of the names of all of the seven dwarfs to distract herself—there was always one she couldn't remember; now, which one was it? Scrunching her nose up while she concentrated didn't help. Nope still couldn't get him. Elusive seventh dwarf! She sighed again.

'Huff all you want, Cass. I'm not putting you down.'

The elevator pinged and the doors slid open while she informed him, 'You'll have to put me down eventually. It'll make it a tad difficult to do the basics, lugging me around like a sack of spuds all day.'

When he turned from side to side to search for the plates on the wall that would indicate where her room was, she waved a limp arm. 'That way.'

'Why didn't you call and say you weren't feeling well?'

Because a part of her had been looking forward to seeing him again, that was why. Her curiosity had been getting the better of her ever since his e-mail had arrived. Only natural considering their history, she'd told herself. What girl *wasn't* fascinated by how her first love looked years after the last time she saw him? It was one of those things that never completely went away. Along with the associated paranoia of wondering whether time had built her memories of him into some kind of magical figure he couldn't possibly live up to, or whether he would have aged much better than she had.

In the face of further humiliation, she lied, 'I felt better when I got up.'

'Liar.'

Cassidy sighed louder than before. 'I *hate* that you can still do that. Fine, then—I wanted to know why I was here.'

'Yes, obviously. Because I didn't explain it in the e-mails I sent you…'

Was he fishing? She lifted her chin and frowned up at his profile at the exact moment he chose to lower his dense lashes and look down at her. It made her breath catch in her lungs. One man should *not* look that good! It took every ounce of strength she had not to drop her gaze to his mouth. Then she had to dig deeper to make herself breathe normally again.

She should never have made the trip over. 'It wasn't like you picked up a phone to discuss it.'

Broad shoulders shrugged before he slotted her key card into the door. 'Different time zones. And my schedule has been crazy.'

Cassidy lifted a brow. 'Liar.'

'Nope.' He shouldered the door open. 'You're seven hours behind over there. I've been dealing with a movie that's running over budget every second. Any time I had to call you would have been during school hours your end. Plus, if you were worried about making the trip and *wanted* me to call you, you'd have said so in your e-mails— wouldn't you?'

She hated it when he used reasoning on her. And when she couldn't read him the way he did her. Back in the good old days the former had been useful mid-debate, and the latter had been endearing as heck—especially when he'd told her what she was thinking in a husky voice, with his mouth hovering above hers. But now? Now it just kept on making her feel like even more of an idiot than she already did for not realising the physical attraction she'd had for him would be as uncontrollable as it had been before. There was no fighting chemistry. When the pheromones said it worked, it worked. It was up to the brain to list the reasons why it couldn't.

Setting her gently on her feet by the giant bed, he leaned over to drag the covers back before standing tall and letting a small smile loose. 'Take it off.'

'Excuse me?'

He jerked his chin. 'That industrial-strength whatever-it-is you're wearing. What is it with women and those boned things, anyway?'

A squeak of outrage sounded in the base of her sore throat. 'You're unbelievable. Go away.'

'I'll go when you're all tucked up in bed. Anything happens to you within twenty-four hours of hitting L.A. I might feel guilty for bringing you here…'

Somewhere in the growing red mist of her anger came a question that temporarily made her gape at him. *'You* brought me here? I thought the studio brought me here? Are you telling me *you* paid for all of this—the flights and the limo pick-up and the fancy room and everything?'

Say no!

'Yes.'

Uh-oh. Room swaying again. But when his hands grasped her elbows she tugged them away and managed to turn round before she flumped down onto the mattress. Automatically toeing her shoes off her feet, she shook her head and blinked into the middle distance. 'I thought the studio paid for it.'

'They paid for a script. We took the money. Now we have to deliver.'

What had she got herself into? She couldn't be beholden to him. It wasn't as if she had the money to pay him back—not until they were paid the balance of their advance for the last script. Even then. Every cent was precious. There was no guarantee she could start writing again without Will and make money at it. Not that she'd tried the last time…

A crooked forefinger arrived under her chin and lifted it to force her gaze upwards. Then he examined her eyes for the most maddening amount of time while she held her breath. 'You need to sleep. I'll come back later and check up on how you're feeling.'

'You don't have to.'

'Go take that ridiculous thing off while I'm here—in case you pass out again.'

'I won't pass—'

'Humour me.'

Pursing her lips, she reached for her pyjamas from under the soft pillows, pushed to her feet and scowled at him on her way to the bathroom, 'I don't know that I can work with this new bossy Will.' She lifted her chin. 'I don't like him.'

Closing the door with a satisfyingly loud click, she took a second to lean against the wood until the world stopped spinning again. For a long time she'd told herself her life was a mess, but it was a glorious kind of mess. Now she felt very much like dropping the 'glorious' part…

She had to sit on the edge of the bathtub to struggle her way out of everything without another dizzy spell. Then she hid the offending underwear under a pile of towels, in case he decided to use the bathroom before he left. Stupid cold! That was what she got for working in a room full of children—she must have incubated the germs on the plane. So much for being considerate and taking the time to see the children through the last term, postponing her trip by a couple of weeks until the summer holidays. They'd repaid her in germs. Bless them.

'You okay in there?' He sounded as if he was standing right by the door.

When she yanked it open, he was.

'You can go away now.'

Will blocked her exit and took his sweet time looking her over from head to toe and back up again, for the second time in as many hours. Only this time it left her skin tingling with more than the cold sweat from her cold. Just one comment about her two-sizes-too-big pyjamas and he was a dead man.

Then his gaze clashed with hers and her eyes widened. What was *that*?

He stepped back. 'Bed.'

Cassidy made a big deal about making sure she patted the covers down the full length of her legs when she was between the cool cotton sheets. The room was wonderfully cool too. Had he turned on the air-conditioning for her? Then she saw the glass of water on the bedside table, alongside the remote control for the television, a box of tissues and the large folder with all the hotel's numbers in it. He'd thought of everything. It was amazingly considerate, actually. It tempered the sharpness brought on by her humiliation, and her voice was calmer as she snuggled down against the large pile of cushions.

'There. Happy now?'

When she chanced another look at him he had the edges of his dark jacket pushed back and his large hands deep in the pockets of his jeans. He seemed so much larger than she remembered—as if he filled the room. And yet still with those boyishly devastating good looks and that thick head of dark hair, with its upward curls at his nape, and the sharply intelligent eyes that studied her so intensely she felt a need to run and hide…

Half of her silently pleaded with him to go away.

The other half probably wished he'd never left to begin with.

'I'll be back later.'

'You don't need to. Call in the morning if you like. I'll sleep.'

The green of his eyes flashed with determination. 'I'll be back later.'

The balance of power within Cassidy swayed towards 'go away'. 'I won't open the door Will.'

'I know.' He took his hands out of his pockets and backed towards the door, his long legs making the journey in three steps. Then he lifted a hand and casually turned something over between his long fingers like a baton, 'That's why I'm keeping your key card.'

Cassidy could have growled at him. But instead she rolled her eyes as she turned away and punched the pillows into shape, hearing the door click quietly shut behind her. After counting to ten, just to be sure, she fought the need to cry. Oh, how much easier it would be if she could hate him…

He was way out of her league now. *Way out.*

She wanted to go home.

CHAPTER TWO

THE dream was feverish. In the no man's land between deep sleep and consciousness came vivid images that were a mixture of the past, the present and some imaginary point in time real only in her mind. The sheets knotted around her legs felt cumbersome, still heavy, even though she'd long since kicked the blanket to one side and damp strands of her auburn hair were stuck to her cheeks and her forehead.

She felt awful.

But she was old enough and wise enough to know she was at the sweating-it-out stage. She just had to let it run its course and her body would fight it off. It might mean she was looking at a few days holed up in the hotel room, but it wasn't as if it was the worst hotel in the world, was it?

The low light from her bedside lamp shone irritatingly through the backs of her eyelids, and voices sounded from the television she had on low volume to help lull her to sleep. She'd never been particularly good with silence. But then neither was she accustomed to the noises of a busy American hotel. So keeping the TV on had seemed like a plan—especially when she'd discovered a channel that showed the familiar programmes she was used to watching at home. That was why it took a moment for her to drag her mind out of its half-slumber into a cognitive state. The door had to have been knocked on several times by then, she figured—with increasing levels of volume…

'Cass?' It was Will.

She groaned and croaked back at him. 'Go away, Will.'

Please go away. Don't make it worse. Let me die in peace. Then if he wanted to he could come and take her body away and donate it to medical science. She was beyond caring any more.

'I'm coming in.'

The man had no idea when to take a hint! The next thing she knew the door was open and he was walking in, with a large paper bag in his hand. So she did the mature thing and grabbed a pillow to hold over her face with both hands. Maybe she could suffocate herself…

'How's the patient?'

'Not in the mood for company,' she mumbled from under the pillow.

'You have a pillow over your face, so I couldn't quite hear that. Here, let me help you.' He pried her fingers loose and removed the pillow. Then he waited for her to squint up at him through narrowed eyes. 'Hello there.'

Cassidy silently called him a really bad name. 'Please go away Will.'

Setting the pillow on the other side of her head, he laid the backs of his fingers against her forehead and frowned. 'When's the last time you took tablets?'

'I don't know—half an hour after you left…maybe…'

'Time for more.'

Struggling her way into a sitting position, she accepted

the tablets he dropped into her palm and washed them down with what was left of the glass of juice on her side table. Then she set the glass back down and lifted her heavy arms to try and tidy her hair before looking up at him from under her lashes.

'I appreciate what you're doing, Will. I do. *And* whatever it is you've brought me in the paper bag. But I just need to sleep it out. It'll be some kind of freaky twenty-four-hour thing, that's all. I've taken my tablets and had some juice, and now I'm going back to sleep. If you leave a number I'll call you when I wake up. I'm not that bad. Really.'

She then ruined the effect by sneezing with enough force to make it feel as if she'd just blown the top off her aching head. She moaned. Someone should just shoot her.

Will calmly handed her a tissue.

She decided to disgust him to get him to leave, blowing her nose loud enough to alert all shipping routes of an incoming fog.

Will had the gall to look vaguely amused. 'You need to eat something. I brought you chicken noodle soup.'

How *could* he? As he reached a large hand into the bag memory slammed into her frontal lobe and ricocheted down her closing throat, wrapping around her heart so tight it made it difficult to breathe. Because he'd done this before, hadn't he? Only she'd had flu that time. They'd been in the tiny bedsit they'd shared for a while instead of living in halls of residence. As well as bringing her everything she'd needed to feel better, and heating endless pans of chicken noodle soup, he had sat up with her, watched television with her, held her in his arms, smoothed her hair until she fell asleep...

It wasn't that she'd forgotten. It was just that the memory hadn't been so vivid in a long time. There had been so many different memories to overshadow it. Heartbreak had a tendency to do that—taking the best of memories and tingeing them with a hint of painful regret for the fact there wouldn't be more memories made in the future. But right now he *was* adding a new one. One that was surrounded in bittersweetness because it wasn't one she could hold onto the same way as the first.

It hurt.

Removing the lid of the soup carton, he wrapped it in a napkin and handed it to her along with a plastic spoon. 'Here…'

Dampening her lips, she hesitated briefly before reaching for the carton. She had no choice but to slide her fingers over his during the exchange, and a jolt of electricity shot up her arm. Her chest was aching when he slid his fingers away. It would have been easier if he'd just set the carton down. Darn it.

Purposefully she took the spoon from him by grasping the opposite end from his fingers, croaking a low, 'Thank you.'

'You're welcome.' He inclined his head.

When she blew too hard on the soup, and splattered just enough hot liquid on the back of her hand to make her frown, she glanced up at him and found amusement dancing in his eyes again. He truly was the most irritating man in the world.

Then he sat on the edge of the bed and turned towards her. 'If you're not better tomorrow I'll get a doctor to come see you.'

'I don't need a doctor; it's a cold—not bubonic plague.'

'And they say *men* make lousy patients…'

Cassidy shook her head. Then leaned in and blew more gently on her soup to cool it. When she looked up, Will was studying her intently—almost as if he'd never seen her before. It made her sigh for the hundredth time that day. 'What now?'

'You changed your hair.'

The words surprised her, but as usual her sarcasm kicked in. 'Yeah. Women tend to do that a couple of times in eight years. We're fickle that way.'

'Still have a smart mouth, though.'

Which apparently gave him leave to drop his gaze and look at it as she formed another pouting 'O' to blow air on the soup. She immediately pursed her lips in response. When his thick lashes lifted she scowled at him. 'Your good deed is done for the day now. You can go and do whatever it is you normally do at this time of night. Wherever you do it and with whomever you do it.'

'Whomever?' The corners of his mouth tugged again. 'Nice use of the English language. Fishing for details, Cass?'

Cassidy had never wanted to scream so much in all her born days. 'Writers are supposed to have a good grasp of the language. Not that you'd understand that. I spent half our time together correcting your spelling mistakes…'

She really had. It wasn't that he couldn't spell, it was just that sometimes his mind worked faster than his typing fingers.

Then she addressed his cockiness. 'And I'm not fishing. It's none of my business.'

'You could try asking me.'

'I'm sorry. Wasn't "it's none of my business" clear enough?'

'Not the littlest bit curious?'

'Why would I be?'

The beginning of one of *those* smiles started in his eyes. And if it started in his eyes first it was devastating when it made it to his mouth. She *knew.* So she stopped it happening by throwing out somewhat desperate words. 'Even if you're free as a bird it doesn't make any difference. You and me? We're workmates. Business partners, if you like. Barely platonic ones. We're like two people stranded on a desert island who have to make the best of it till the next rescue boat arrives—as good as strangers. You don't know any more about who I am now than I know about—'

'You're babbling. You always babble when you're nervous. Why are you nervous, Cass?'

Screwing up her face, she set the soup carton onto the side table and slid down under the covers, lifting them and tucking them over her head. 'I hate you. Would you *go away*? I'm not up to this. You're still the most annoying man I've ever known.'

'Makes me memorable…'

Cassidy growled, and promptly ended up coughing when the vibration hurt her raw throat. Somewhere mid-cough she heard what sounded like a low chuckle of laughter. She peeked over the edge of the covers ready to scowl at him and found him lifting his brows in a question, a completely unreadable expression on his face. It made her narrow her eyes.

'You know we need to get on better than this to work together, don't you?'

She did, and immediately felt like a fool again. 'Can we try and get on better when I don't feel like the hotel fell on me?'

'When you're weak is probably the best time to talk this through.'

'That's evil.'

Will had more difficulty stifling his smile than he had so far. 'True.'

He wasn't apologising for it, though, was he? The rat. Cassidy tried hard not to be charmed by it; she did. But a small sparkle-eyed smile was apparently nearly as effective as a killer one, and before she knew it she was smiling back at him. Then she shook her head. 'I hate you.'

'Mmm.' He leaned forward, his large body distractingly close to hers and his familiar scent somehow making it through her blocked nose. 'You said.'

When he lifted the soup carton Cassidy lifted her gaze to his hair. He had great hair. The colour of dark chocolate, thick enough to tempt a woman's fingertips, and distinctly male to the touch when she touched it, but soft enough to encourage her to slide her fingers deep... She wished she didn't remember so much...

Will leaned back. 'You need to eat.'

'Bossing me again, Ryan?'

'Necessary, Malone.'

Without comment she went ahead and sipped at the soup, her gaze flickering to his often enough for her to know he was still watching her. Not that she needed to look to confirm it. She'd always known when Will was looking at her. In the same way she could feel the newfound tension lying between them.

Thick lashes blinked lazily at even intervals, and then he asked, 'Good?'

'Mmm-hmm.' She nodded. *'Good.'*

Looking around the room for a moment, Will folded his dark brows in thought before he took a deep breath and focused on her again. 'I think you should stay at my place while you're in L.A.'

Cassidy almost choked on her soup. He had a knack of doing that to her. But he couldn't be serious! There was no way she could go and stay at his place—be under the same roof with him twenty-four-seven. They were barely managing to make civil conversation between his short sentences and her loose tongue. And now he wanted them somewhere they couldn't escape from each other? Oh, yeah. That would help.

Then she thought about the fact he was paying for the hotel room she was in and felt guilty. Maybe if she found a computer and checked her meager bank account she could discover somewhere cheap and cheerful to stay? It didn't need to be fancy: a bed, a door that locked, a shower, a minimal number of cockroaches...

Will continued while she blinked at him, 'We need to spitball ideas and get to work. And we never used to stick to a nine to five, so if we're working through the night it makes sense to be somewhere we can do that. I'll come get you in the morning.'

Cassidy wondered if there was ever going to be a point where she got to make decisions on her own. 'Don't you have an office?'

'I have one we can work in at home, yes.'

Not what she'd meant, and he knew it. 'In the city. You can't run an entire production company from home.'

'I probably could. But, yes, I do have offices in the city. Still the same problem there—this makes more sense.'

It didn't matter if it made sense. Surely he remembered that about her? But before she could even string together a thought, never mind form the words to argue it out, he was pushing to his feet. 'While you're not feeling well you can take a break to sleep any time you need to. I'll come get you at nine.'

Cassidy watched him get halfway to the door before she managed to open her mouth. 'I'm not comfortable with the idea of living in your house—or apartment—or whatever it is you have.'

'You'll forget that when you've been there a few days.'

'Damn it, Will!' She frowned at him when he turned round. 'You can't keep riding roughshod over me like this. If I don't want to stay in your house I don't have to. And if it's because you're paying for this hotel then I can find somewhere—'

Lowering his chin, he lifted his brows with amused disbelief. 'You think paying for this room is a problem for me?'

'That's not the point. Whether or not you can afford—'

Will shook his head, smiling incredulously. 'It's got nothing to do with money. It's got to do with practicality. *Man.* I'd forgotten how stubborn you can be.'

Swallowing down another pang of hurt that he'd forgotten *anything* about her when she remembered everything about him, Cassidy arched a brow. 'Pot, meet kettle. Regardless of whether or not you can afford to pay for this room, the simple fact is you shouldn't be. I'll pay you back whatever you've already forked out. I don't want to owe you anything. This is business and we both know it. Whatever we once had doesn't matter any more. We're not even friends now.'

'And blunt. That part I hadn't forgotten.' He lifted his chin and frowned at a random point in the air while taking a deep breath that expanded his wide chest. Then he dropped his chin and looked her straight in the eye. 'You're right. It *is* business. You have a job back home. I have a job here. So the sooner we get this done the sooner we can get back to work. If we dig in, and eat, drink and sleep this script for the next few weeks, we can nail it.'

It was all about the script; of course it was.

Will quirked his brows. 'Well?'

'It's business.'

'Exactly.'

'Right.' She didn't have the energy to keep fighting with him. 'Fine, then.'

With his mouth drawn into a thin line and a frown darkening his face, Will swung round and tugged on the door. 'Nine o'clock.'

When the door closed behind him Cassidy blinked at it. For a brief second he'd almost looked angry. How on earth were they supposed to communicate well enough to write a script if they couldn't even hold a conversation? She flumped further down on the pillows and put what was left of her soup on the nightstand before tugging the covers up over her shoulders. She felt cold again, she was shivery— and suddenly she had an incredible sense of loneliness to add to her feeling homesick.

Her first trip to Hollywood should be a fairytale experience. It was a dream she'd had since childhood, when the magic of movies had sucked her into the kind of imaginary worlds that had enthralled her for most of her life. Everything about it had fascinated her as she got older: the sets, the effects, the lighting, the locations, where the words the actors and actresses spoke came from. The latter had then become something she wanted to do—she wanted to put those words there. To watch a movie on a big screen and hear words she had written on a flat page spoken by an actor or actress who could add depths and nuances she might never even have thought of.

When she'd got her dream the world had become the most amazing place to her. And she'd got to share that magic with the man she loved. It had been perfect. She had been so happy.

But there was no such thing as perfect happiness. Life had taught her that. Failure had taken the sparkly-eyed wonder from her eyes. Then she'd had to give up her dreams, her confidence shattered, her heart broken, because Will had gone and she'd had no choice but to watch him walk away. The last time she had seen him was indelibly imprinted on her brain, and in the empty part of her heart that had died that day...

Cassidy had felt as if all the magic had been sucked out of her life. And she'd never got it back. Just small pockets of happiness ever since. But then that was everyone's life, she had told herself. She just needed to get on with it. One day after another.

Even if for a very, very brief moment on her flight over she'd allowed herself to dream again. Not so much of Will, but of the other great love she'd lost. She'd foolishly allowed herself to think about what might happen if she rediscovered her muse and decided to take a chance in Hollywood for a while. But this script was simply something to get out of the way. Then she would go home. End of story. No pun intended.

Then she would have to decide what she wanted to do with the rest of her life.

At nine she'd been in the foyer for ten minutes, glad of the concierge to help her with her bags and glad at how easy checking out proved to be. Still a little light headed, she found a plump cushioned chair and waited…

Will was outside at the stroke of nine. Something else that was new about him. He'd once been the worst time-keeper she'd ever known.

'You'll be late for your own funeral,' she would tell him.

'Ah, now, that's the one time I can guarantee I'll be on time,' he would tease back with a smile.

Cassidy missed that Will.

The new Will was frowning behind his designer sun-glasses the second he got out of his lowslung silver sports car. He said something to the uniformed man in charge of valet parking as he slipped him a folded bill, then pushed through the doors and removed his sunglasses before seeking her out. Four steps later he had his hand on the handle of her case.

'Did you check out?'

'Yes.'

'Any problems?'

'No. They said it was taken care of.'

With a nod he stepped back, watching her rise. 'Feeling any better?'

It was said with just enough softness in his deep voice to make it sound as if he cared, which made Cassidy feel the need to sigh again. Instead she managed a small smile as she stood. 'Yes. Thank you.'

Somewhere in the wee small hours of the night she had decided the best way not to be so physically aware of Will's presence was to avoid looking at him whenever possible. So she didn't make eye contact as she waited for him to load her case into the boot of his car. Instead she smiled at the liveried valet as he opened the passenger door for her—though she did almost embarrass herself again by trying to get in the wrong side of the car...

When Will got into the driver's seat and buckled up she looked out of the side window to watch Rodeo Drive starting to think about coming to life. But they had barely pulled away from the hotel before he took advantage of the fact she was trapped.

'Want to tell me what's *really* bothering you about staying at my place?'

Not so much. No. She puffed her cheeks out for a second and controlled her errant tongue before answering. 'We don't know each other that well any more. It's going be like spending time in a stranger's house.'

There was a brief silence, then; 'I disagree.'

Well, now, there was a surprise. They worked their way through intersections and filtered into traffic while Cassidy noticed all the differences that indicated she was in a different country from home. Larger cars, palm trees, billboards advertising things she'd never heard of before, different shaped traffic lights...

Will kept going. 'We're not strangers. People don't change that much.'

She begged to differ. And if she hadn't had living proof

in herself then she had it in the man sitting so close to her in the confined space of what she now knew was a Mustang something-or-other—she'd seen a little tag somewhere. Not that she was going to turn her head to look for it again, if it meant she might end up catching a glimpse of him from her peripheral vision. Just being so close to him, so aware of every breath he took and every movement of his large hands or long legs, was enough for her to deal with, thanks very much.

'Yes, they do. Life changes them. Experiences change them…' She had a sudden brainwave. 'It's exactly the kind of problem Nick and Rachel will have when they meet again.'

The mention of their fictional characters momentarily silenced Will. Then she heard him take a breath and let it out. 'That's true.'

So it was true for their fictional characters but not for them? How did *that* work? It was enough to make her turn her head and aim a suspicious sideways glance at his general gorgeousness. 'It's not like they're going to trust each other either.'

'Well, she did steal the artifact from him.'

'No—she took it to give it back to its rightful owners. There's a difference. He'd have sold it on the open market for whatever he could get.'

'She lived off the money they made doing the same thing in the past. You can't use that as an argument against him.'

'Oh? Now we're saying there has to be moral equivalency?'

Will shot her a quick yet intense gaze as they waited in traffic, his deep voice somehow more intense within the car's interior. 'It's not the best plan to alienate everyone to the hero and heroine before we even get started, is it? There are always two sides to every story. You want to make him into a bad boy then you have to make the audience understand why his morals are lower than hers.'

'Bad heroes sell. You can't tell me they don't. Bad heroines are universally hated.' Cassidy lifted her chin, but she could feel the smile forming on her face. It was like one of their debates of old. 'Unless you're thinking of turning her evil—which, incidentally, you'll do over my dead body. The audience needs to empathise with her. That'll sell.'

'Actually, I can tell you exactly what sells these days. Right now its superheroes and family-friendly.' His long fingers flexed against the steering wheel. 'The real money can be found in family-oriented movies, where good is good and bad is bad. It's black and white. Moral equivalency needn't apply. Last year seven films with a G or PG rating earned more than one hundred million at the domestic box office, and three PG-rated films were among the year's top ten earners. Only one R-rated film was in the ten top grossing films—and there was no moral equivalency in that movie, I can assure you.'

The smile on her face faded and was replaced with blinking surprise as he recited it all in an even tone, negotiating increasing traffic at the same time. It seemed everyone in Los Angeles had a car.

He knew his stuff, didn't he? Who was she to argue? Not that it stopped her. 'Correct me if I'm wrong, but haven't you just proved my point on moral equivalency?'

Silence. Then to her utter astonishment a burst of laughter—deep, rumbling, oh-so-very-male laughter—

then a wry smile and a shake of his head. 'It's been a long time since anyone spoke to me the way you do.'

Cassidy blinked some more. 'Maybe people should do it more often.'

'If they did they'd get fired more often.'

The corners of her mouth tugged upwards. 'Wow. Who knew you were a tyrant in the making, back in the day?'

'I'm not a tyrant.' He seemed surprised she thought he was.

'No?' Turning a little more towards him, she leaned her back against the passenger door and angled her head in question. 'What are you, then?'

'The boss.'

'So no one can correct you when you're wrong?'

'They can put forward a different point of view, if that's what you mean.' He was forced to break eye contact with her to concentrate on where they were going. 'No one ever does it the way you do, though.'

Cassidy couldn't help but allow the chuckle of laugher forming in her chest to widen her smile. 'So no one actually looks you in the eye and tells you you're wrong?'

'Not in so many words, no.'

No wonder he'd got so arrogant over the years. If no one ever stood up to him, or gave as good as they got, it would be a breeding ground for arrogance. Irrationally, it made her feel sorry for him. Everyone needed someone who cared enough about them to be brutally honest when it was needed. No one was ever right one hundred percent of the time, after all. Being blunt on the odd occasion to demonstrate another point of view showed you cared enough about them to try and save them from the kind of mistakes arrogance might make. To Cassidy,

knowing no one did that for Will made him seem very…
alone…

'She'll probably feel awkward when she sees him again.'

Huh? Oh, he meant Rachel, didn't he? Right—script stuff. Stay with the flow of conversation, Cassidy. 'I doubt she'd have sought him out voluntarily.'

'So we need something that brings them together.'

Cassidy arched a brow. 'You're going to want him to rescue her, aren't you?'

The one corner of his full mouth she could see hitched upwards. 'Who doesn't like it when the hero swoops in to rescue the heroine?'

'*Sexist.* Why can't the heroine rescue the hero? Or rescue herself? Or just be in the same place as him searching for something when they *both* get in trouble and have to work *together* to get out of it…?'

Will shot a brief, sparkle eyed glance her way. 'Okay, then. He has to rescue her from something when they end up in the same place hunting for something.'

Cassidy rolled her eyes. 'Fine. But I'm fighting for a later scene when *she* has to rescue *him* right back.'

'We're not making Nick look weak.'

'Vulnerable—not weak. Women find vulnerability sexy in a strong male. You should try it some time. Might get you a girlfriend…' The reappearance of her errant tongue made her groan inwardly and avoid his gaze when he looked her way again.

'You don't know I don't have a girlfriend.'

'I told you, it's none of my—'

'I don't have one right now. But all you had to do was ask.'

Oh, for crying out loud. Not only had she just caused a

self-inflicted wound at the idea of him with another woman, but now he'd managed to slip that little piece of unwanted information into the conversation it was only a matter of time before—

'What about you?'

Yep. There it was. Well, if he thought for one single, solitary second she was discussing the disastrous attempts she had eventually made at having a love life—long, *long* after he'd left—then he had another think coming. Not that it would be a long conversation.

Lifting her chin, she smiled sweetly. 'I don't have a girlfriend either.'

Will chuckled for the second time.

The sound was ridiculously distracting to her. How did it do that? It wasn't as if she hadn't heard him laugh before; she'd heard him chuckle, laugh softly, laugh out loud—had felt the rumble in his chest and been in his arms when his body had shaken with the reverberations. She knew how the light would dance in his eyes, how he would smile the amazingly infectious smile that gave everyone around him no choice but to smile along with him. For a long time Cassidy had believed she'd fallen for his laughter first. Yes, his boyish looks, height, gorgeous hair, etc., etc. might have been what had initially caught her eye. But it had been the sound of his laughter and the first glimpse of *that* smile that had drawn her heart to him.

Since she'd got to Los Angeles she'd wondered if she'd imagined the effect his laughter had on her. As if her memories were tangled up on some mythical pedestal she might have elevated him to over the years. But it was having exactly the same effect on her as before: skin tingling, chest warming—as if the sound had somehow reached out and physically touched her...

Forcing her gaze away, she turned forward in the seat to look out through the windscreen, and was surprised to see the ocean beside them. 'Where are we?'

'Pacific Coast Highway. It's the equivalent of Malibu's main street.'

'Malibu?'

'It's where I live.'

It was? Malibu? Where the rich and famous lived? She knew he'd done well since he came to California, but that he'd done well enough to be able to afford—

'It was originally part of the territory of the Chumash Nation of Native Americans. They called it Humaliwo— or "the surf sounds loudly". The current name derives from that. but the "Hu" syllable isn't stressed...' When she gaped at him he looked away from the highway long enough to raise his brows at her. 'What?'

'Who *are* you?'

The question was out before she could stop it, her words low and filled with incredulity. It was just the more he said the less she felt she knew him; it was as if he had somehow morphed into a completely different person when he'd moved halfway across the planet—and it was just so at odds with the many things that were familiar to her that it left her feeling a little...*lost*...

Will checked the road again, then looked back at her. 'You know me, Cass.'

His saying it in a low rumble that made goosebumps break out on her skin and her heart do a kind of weird twisting move in her chest only made her study him even more intently. 'How do you know all this stuff?'

'About Malibu?'

'It's like you've swallowed an encyclopaedia since you got here. Hollywood-speak, movie industry stats, local history…'

What looked almost like confusion flickered across the green of his eyes before he turned his head to watch the road again. 'Hollywood speak is everyday language here. Movie stats I study as part of my job, and Malibu I just happen to like—it's why I moved here the minute I could afford it. I hate the city.'

Actually, the last part she understood. Home of Disneyland and movie stars, Beverly Hills and Hollywood, she knew Los Angeles had long lured people into its glittering fantasy world, with its endless sunshine, palm trees, shopping malls and beautiful people. The city was like no place she'd ever been before. But after so many years dreaming about it, she'd known in less than twenty-four hours that she couldn't live there. Not in the city anyway. Too many people, too many cars, too much smog. No one saying hello to their fellow human beings in the street unless they were dressed as iconic movie figures and demanding money in exchange for a photograph with them. Cassidy had taken one afternoon to wander along Hollywood Boulevard, and as fascinating as it had been, reading the iconic stars beneath her feet, it hadn't made her feel at home. And now she'd discovered Will possibly felt that way too…

Well, it gave them some common ground, didn't it? A stretch maybe, but she would take what she could get…

Despite the danger, Cassidy wanted to know more. Her dilemma became whether or not to actually *ask* any more. If she did she would be getting a window into his life—

would have new Will Ryan memories to add to the cornu-copia of old ones she already carried around with her. If somewhere along the way the new version of him proved as addictive as the old? Well, then she was in big, *big* trouble…

Who was she kidding? Cassidy had always been one of those people that needed to know. Christmas presents—she shook them. Books—she read the last pages before she got halfway through them. Favourite TV shows—she trawled the internet looking for spoilers for a new series before the episodes made it to the screen. There was about as much chance of her not asking as—

'So tell me more about Malibu.'

'What do you want to know?'

'Whatever you decide to tell me…'

She looked out through the windscreen at the glittering aquamarine blue of the Pacific Ocean, the thrill of seeing it for the first time bringing a soft smile to her mouth. She had always loved the ocean. Not surprising, really, when she lived on a tiny island surrounded by it. But there was just something about the ebb and flow of the tide…as if it was the subliminal heartbeat of the planet. Every time she saw the sea it made her smile. Seeing the Pacific for the first time was like meeting a new friend.

'That's the Pacific. Beautiful, isn't she?'

'She is.' Cassidy allowed herself to wonder why anything associated with the sea was always a 'she'. Probably something to do with moods and unpredictabil-ity and seduction, she supposed. From that point of view it was easy to see why seafaring men of old would have chosen the feminine to describe her.

'Malibu hugs the Pacific north of Santa Monica. It

has over twenty miles of coastline. Surfing is the big thing, obviously—endless opportunities for catching the perfect wave…'

The smile she could hear in his voice made her turn to look at his strong profile; the flicker of his thick dark lashes as he watched the traffic was unbelievably hypnotic to her.'You surf?'

The corner of his mouth tugged. 'Used to. Don't have as much time now…'

A sudden visual image of Will walking out of the surf, glistening with water and shaking his head to loosen silvery droplets from his thick hair while he smiled *that* smile, did all sorts of delicious things to Cassidy's libido and left her mouth unbearably dry. There were times her active imagination took on a life of its own—useful in writerly terms, but not so useful when she was supposed to be thinking in terms of Will as a business partner. There could be no thinking of him bare-chested. Or towelling his hair for him. Or lying down on a large blanket beside him on warm sand.

Goodness, it was hot all of a sudden…

'It's part of the reason I bought a house on the beach.'

Suddenly staying at his house was looking more attractive to her. But… 'You bought a house on the beach so you could surf more, and then quit surfing? That makes perfect sense.'

He shrugged. 'Just the way it worked out.'

The house they pulled up in front of looked small and cosy. The sound of the ocean filled her ears as she stepped outside into warm salty air that made her breathe deep and appreciate the difference in air quality after the lack of oxygen in Los Angeles. But when Will unlocked the front door and stepped back to allow her to go ahead of him her eyes widened. Okay, it wasn't small and cosy. Will's house was… Well, it was amazing…

The deceptive frontage on the road made it look like it was just the one storey, and not all that big, when in fact it was split level and stretched for miles, with its lower level suspended above golden sands outside so that the huge picture windows made it look as if the entire house was floating above the waves. Open-plan, rich wooden floors, sparse furniture that didn't take anything from the views. It was very male, very modern, but stunningly beautiful.

It yelled *money* from every corner.

When Cassidy hovered at the top of the stairs, Will closed the front door and stepped over beside her. 'The view sold it.'

'Well, it would, wouldn't it?'

'Kitchen, living room, gym, home cinema and office are all on the lower level. Your room is over here to the left.' He took her case in that direction while she continued staring out of the windows.

Now she knew why Lizzie had fallen for Pemberley before she fell for Darcy. Because the part of Cassidy's soul that loved the ocean could live happily ever after in a house like Will's. Give or take a few feminine touches. If *she* lived there she would have bright comfy cushions on the large sofas, flowers in vases, books on the almost empty shelves where pieces of modern art were displayed. She could picture it in her mind's eye. She could practically hear music playing from an invisible stereo, laughter echoing off the walls, and the sound of small, running bare feet coming in from the beach. It made her heart hurt. How dared he have the house of her dreams? It was as if he'd purposely gone out and stolen every dream she'd ever had and held it from her, to add to breaking her heart the way he had.

She genuinely hated him for that.

With a deep breath she turned on her heel and followed Will along the hall that skirted the floor below, rolling her eyes when she got to the open doorway and looked in at the bedroom she would be staying in. Of course it had the same ocean view. And naturally Will was sliding open the glass windows so the sea breeze caught the light curtains. Was there ever any doubt it would have its own balcony, with comfy lounge chairs just waiting to be occupied so she could watch the sunset at the end of the day?

Stepping into a little corner of heaven, she plunked down on the end of the large bed and allowed herself to bounce just once on the deep mattress while she fought the need to cry. It really wasn't fair. How *could* he? What had she ever done to him to deserve this kind of torture?

Will turned from the windows and pushed his hands deep into the pockets of his dark jeans as he studied her. 'Tired?'

Weary would have been a better word, she felt. 'A little. Coffee would probably help. And I should take some tablets again, just in case.'

'Okay.' He nodded. 'Did you have breakfast?'

'No.'

'Yeah, that'll help you get better. Will bagels and lox do?'

'Depends.' Cassidy lifted her chin, stifled a wry smile and arched a brow. 'What is lox, exactly?'

His eyes sparkled. 'It's smoked salmon. Bagels with cream cheese and smoked salmon.'

'Ahh.'

'Is that "Yes, Will"?'

A more genuine smile broke free as she inclined her head. 'Yes, Will. Thank you. Bagels and lox sounds lovely.'

As if to emphasise her approval her stomach growled softly, making Will's mouth twitch as he left the room. 'Come down when you're ready. Feed a cold and all that…'

She wished he would stop being nice. Annoying Will her heart could cope with. But if he started adding Nice Will to the house she'd fallen in love with at first sight she would be in even bigger trouble than she had been twenty-four hours ago.

Lying back on the bed, she turned her head and closed her eyes, breathing as deep as her aching chest would allow while she compared Will's life to the one she had. It wasn't hard to see who had fared better. If her self-confidence had been low before she'd stepped on the plane in Dublin, it was pretty much sitting at the bottom of a dark pit of despair now. She really needed to do something that would make her feel like herself again. But that was just it. Since Will, she'd never really discovered who Cassidy Malone was without him. Maybe it was time to find out?

After all, she was in the house of her dreams in California, a stone's throw away from the industry she still found completely absorbing—even from the periphery, as a viewer of the art form. It was a step in the right direction, wasn't it? Nothing ventured, nothing gained?

She slapped her palms against the cool covers and sat upright, reaching into her bag for her tablets and taking them with her as she left the room. Coffee, bagels and lox, tablets—and then she was going to start work and see if she still re-membered how to write. That was somewhere to start…

CHAPTER THREE

'THAT'S the most ridiculous thing I've ever heard.'

'How is it?'

'How is it *not*?' She blinked incredulously at him, then continued looking around the large glass desk for the pen she knew she'd had five minutes ago. 'You want them to find a hidden nuclear warhead in the middle of an archaeological dig?'

Will allowed a pen to twirl between his thumb and forefinger, as if teasing her with it because she couldn't find her own. 'We need explosions.'

'A nuclear warhead is a little more than a simple explosion. And how on earth did the terrorist group get the thing down there, when we've already said that no one has discovered the site after centuries of searching?' Cassidy shook her head, lifting discarded scene cards in her search.

'We can change that. It's one line.' His pen stilled and his deep voice informed her, 'Behind your ear.'

'What?' She scowled at him, her pulse hitching when she realised how intensely he was staring at her as he lounged in his chair and swung it from side to side. That chair had been driving her crazy. It had a squeak. She'd have thought a man of Will's means could afford a can of oil to fix something that irritating, but *no*. He just kept swinging and squeaking, and swinging and squeaking, until she thought she might have to kill him.

He jerked his chin at her. 'Your pen. It's behind your ear.'

When she reached up her hand she sighed; of course it was.

Retrieving the pen from behind her ear, she reached for the last card he'd scrawled notes on and scribbled through half of it forcefully. 'Rachel wouldn't be seen dead wearing *that* either. You're turning her into a sex object.'

The chair squeaked back and forth. 'Bad boy hero, sexy heroine, explosions, treasure hunt, hint of romance—all the ingredients of a blockbuster, trust me…'

'The box office is all that matters to you, is it?' Cassidy began rhythmically tapping the end of her pen on the glass tabletop. 'Forget telling a story, or little things such as character arc and continuity.'

'We're still at the brainstorming stage. We're miles away from character arc and continuity. This is the fun part.'

Really? Because Cassidy hadn't noticed the 'fun part' so much. It was almost as if Will was determined to get her to argue with him. Surely a man with his experience in the business knew better than to fall into the usual traps of cliché and plot device? If she didn't know better she might say he was playing with her on purpose…

While she considered the possibility of that with narrowed eyes, she tapped her pen harder and faster against the glass. Will continued to add to the ambient noise with the squeaking of his chair.

Then his mouth twitched and he nodded at her pen. 'That could get irritating after a while…'

'You think?' She lifted her brows and tapped the pen harder. 'Like the squeaking of your chair, perhaps?'

When she pouted there was a split second of silence as the tapping and the squeaking stopped. Then, out of nowhere, they both laughed at the same time. Cassidy tossed the pen down, running her palms over her face as she groaned loudly. The man was making her *insane*!

Residual laughter sounded in the deep rumble of Will's voice. 'Time for a break.'

It only occurred to her that his voice sounded closer when warm hands closed over hers to lift them from her face, and she found herself tilting her chin up to look into the green of his gaze. He was gorgeous. Take-a-girl's-breath-away gorgeous. Her heart thundered against her breastbone loud enough for her to hear it in her ears as he smiled a small smile that darkened his eyes a shade, then lowered her hands before stepping back and gently tugging her upright.

'I need food.'

'Again? We ate less than an hour ago.' There had been sandwiches. Cassidy definitely remembered there being sandwiches.

'Five hours ago.'

It was? She looked out of the windows as Will turned, keeping hold of one of her wrists to draw her towards the door. Sure enough, outside the light was changing, the tide was turning and people were beginning to—

Hang on a minute. *Why* did Will still have hold of her wrist?

Turning her head, she dropped her chin and frowned down at the human handcuff. Long fingers were lightly hooked over her pulse-point, but they were hooked never-theless, and he was walking them through the living area towards the kitchen. She couldn't take a chance on him re-alising what he did to her pulse. So she gently twisted her wrist and reclaimed it, frowning all the harder at the fact her skin still tingled where he had touched.

Will glanced briefly over his shoulder, then walked to the giant refrigerator and looked inside. 'Steaks okay with you? We can flame-grill them on the deck.'

'Sounds more than fine with me.' She stopped at the end of the narrow breakfast bar and rested her palms on the granite surface. 'What can I do to help?'

'Chop some salad, if you like. Use whatever you fancy out of the fridge.'

Cassidy forgot herself and smiled as he reappeared, tossed the steaks down on the counter and reached into a drawer for barbecue utensils. 'You have the weirdest ac-cent now, you know. Tang of American, but still using Irish phrases.'

A brief sideways glance of sparkle-eyed amusement was aimed her way. 'You can take the boy out of Ireland…'

She rolled her eyes.

Will jerked his dark brows as he unwrapped the steaks. 'Everyone does it. You spend time in a certain environ-ment, surrounded by people who talk a certain way, and you absorb some of it. It's probably a subliminal need for acceptance.'

The idea that a man like Will would feel the need for acceptance anywhere momentarily baffled Cassidy. Maybe she was reading too much into it? She was known to do that. A lot of women were. She stepped towards the fridge to have a poke around for salad ingredients. 'Was it weird at first? Living here, I mean?'

'In Malibu or in California?'

When he reached past her for a bottle of sauce Cassidy's breathing hitched. He'd bent his upper body over hers, had reached his arm over her shoulder and brushed his finger-tips against her hair on the way past, surrounding her for a fleeting moment with an intensely male body heat that contrasted so very sharply with the cold air from the re-frigerator's interior. It had an immediate visceral reaction on her. Goosebumps broke out on her skin, her abdomen tensed, her breasts grew heavy. She even had to swallow hard to dampen her dry mouth and close her eyes to stifle a low moan.

For crying out loud—she knew it had been a long time since she'd last made love, but it was really no excuse for the compulsive need she suddenly felt to turn round and launch herself at him, so they could spend several hours seeing if they still remembered how to play each other's bodies like fine instruments...

One, two, three breaths of cool, refrigerated air—then she reappeared from behind the door with an iceberg lettuce, tomatoes, a cucumber, and two different bottles of salad dressing. When she chanced a sideways glance at Will she found him on the other side of the breakfast bar, studying her intently.

'Malibu or California?'

'What?'

'You asked was it weird living here. I asked Malibu or California.'

Oh, yes, that was right. She had done that. 'California.'

'Yes.'

She set her things on the counter and lifted a brow. 'Malibu?'

'No.'

When light danced across his eyes she knew he was messing with her, so she shook her head. 'A bowl for this stuff?'

'Second cupboard on the left, underneath you.'

'So why was California weird?' She opened the cupboard and hunched down to look inside.

'Why don't you hit me with *your* first impressions and I'll tell you if I felt the same way when I got here…' The sound of doors sliding told her he had moved towards the deck.

By the time she came back up, with a large wooden bowl in hand, he was firing up the outdoor grill. So she found a knife and a chopping board all on her own, while raising her voice to continue the conversation. 'Way more people, nobody smiles and says hello the way they do at home, hotter, brighter—drier. Nothing as green as you'd see in Ireland. Food's different, television is different, the cars people drive are different… Some things are familiar, but the vast majority of differences outshadow them…'

Will was smiling yet another small smile as he came back in, the sea breeze outside having created unruly waves in his dark hair that made him look even more boyish than he already did in his simple white T-shirt and blue jeans combo. No one would ever look at the man and put him in his early thirties. Good genetics, Cassidy supposed. His kids would inherit that anti-ageing gene, and the boys would all look like him, wouldn't they? With dark hair that even when tamed would rebel, with that outward flick at the nape, and green eyes that sparkled with amusement, and the charm of the devil when they wanted something, and—

Cassidy couldn't believe she was standing in his beautiful house and picturing dozens of mini-Wills standing between them. She'd be naming them next. Maybe her biological clock was kicking in?

'In other words weird…'

She smiled as she chopped. 'Okay. Point taken. So why is Malibu different?'

'It's not so crowded here. The air's better.' He shrugged his shoulders as he turned bottles of wine on a rack to read the labels. 'Quieter. More private. I'd lived in California long enough by the time I bought this place that it wasn't so alien to me any more. But this was the first place I felt I could call home.'

'You don't see Ireland as home any more?'

'I see it as where I come from, and a part of who I am, but I have my life in California now.'

Cassidy had known that for a long time. But hearing him say it didn't make it any easier. It was another thing that highlighted how different they were. Somehow she knew she would always see Ireland as home. She had thirty years' worth of memories there—not all of them good, granted. But it was the good and the bad that made her who she was—for better or worse. A part of her would always ache for the green, green grass of home if she left it behind. The fact Will had left *everything* behind without any apparent sense of poignancy made her wonder if he remembered their time together the same way she did. Or remembered that he had said he loved her.

Maybe the harsh truth was he hadn't. Not the way she had loved him. If he had he would never have left her, would he?

The sound of a cork popping brought her gaze back to him as he set a bottle of red wine on the counter to breathe. But when he reached for deep bowled glasses and she opened her mouth to remind him of the dangers of her errant tongue and alcohol, he surprised her.

'Why teaching?' he asked.

She frowned in confusion. 'What?'

'Why teaching?' He turned around and leaned back against the counter, folding his arms across his chest and studying her with hooded eyes. 'I don't remember you ever showing an interest in it when I knew you before.'

Well, no, because when he'd known her she'd still had dreams that felt as if they were within her grasp. Then she'd been given a harsh reality check. She shrugged and tossed the chopped-up salad ingredients in the bowl. 'Necessity to start with, I guess. I needed a job with a regular wage. If I was going to spend a good portion of my life working, it made sense to me to be doing something I might enjoy…'

'Do you?'

'Do I what?'

'Enjoy it?'

'I'd enjoy it more if I was better paid.' She shot him a brief smile, then concentrated on reading the labels on the salad dressings. 'I like little kids. They think in straight lines. They still believe in magic. Adults get the magic knocked out of them with age. Every day when I spend time with a classroom full of kids, and they do or say or discover something that makes me smile, I get a little of that magic back for a minute.'

When he remained silent, curiosity made her turn her head so she could try and read his expression. He was still staring at her, thick lashes still at half-mast so she couldn't see his eyes properly. It was disconcerting.

Then he tugged on a ragged corner of her heart with a low, rumbled comment. 'You used to believe in magic more than anyone I'd ever met…'

Cassidy felt a hard lump forming in her throat, and immediately felt the need to turn her face away, dropping her chin and hiding behind a strand of hair that had escaped from her up-do as she tried to open the lid of the salad dressing. 'Like I said. It gets knocked out of you with age.'

Was this lid cemented on? She pursed her lips and felt the cap digging into her palm as she tried twisting it with a little more force, shifting her shoulder so she was literally putting her back into it, while forcing words out through tight lips at the same time.

'Just part—of life—that's all. Nobody's fault. Or any—'

A large hand settled lightly over her fingers and Cassidy's chin snapped up. He gently removed the bottle from her hand and opened it with one deft twist of his wrist. Then he held it out for her, warmth shining from his eyes and the corners of his mouth tugging upwards. 'Borderline babbling again, Malone.'

Sighing heavily, she reached for the bottle. 'You're the one in charge of the magic these days—industry of dreams and all that. Maybe I handed on the baton.'

Will's head lowered closer to hers, his voice dropping an octave. 'You're saying I couldn't make magic back in the day?' Apparently it was enough to bring one of *those* smiles her way. 'I think my ego might be bruised.'

That wasn't the kind of magic she'd meant. But before she could form a coherent sentence he turned away, lifting the steaks from the counter-top and walking out onto the deck. Leaving Cassidy staring through the glass at him and feeling distinctly confused. Her inability to read him was really starting to bug her.

Once the steaks were on the fancy stainless steel grill he had on the deck, Will closed the lid and came back to the open door, leaning on the frame and studying her before he took a deep breath and asked, 'How are you feeling?'

'Better.' She smiled before turning to put away everything she hadn't used. 'I've stayed upright for more than twenty-four hours now—go me.'

'How do you feel about a trip tomorrow?'

Cassidy's eyes narrowed with suspicion. 'Where to?'

'Magic land…'

Leaning forward in her seat on the golf cart, Cassidy couldn't help but grin like an idiot at her surroundings. It was better than Christmas as far as she was concerned.

'You want to stop and take a look around?'

Yes! She turned to nod enthusiastically at Will. *'Please.'*

It might have seemed like an ordinary street to some people, but to Cassidy it really was magic land. From the second they'd pulled up at the studio's parking lot it had been nigh on impossible to keep the smile off her face. She'd dreamed about places like this for most of her life— but to actually be there…

To Will, visiting the back lots of a studio was probably like taking a busman's holiday, but there wasn't a single thing that Cassidy didn't find fascinating, with an almost child-like glee. Every large warehouse structure they passed was the cover of a storybook waiting to be opened; every extra in full costume was someone she wanted to talk to; every truck full of props was an adventure playground. And the streets of the back lot, with houses and storefronts and windows and open doorways, were just calling out for fictional characters to live there and tell their stories. Cassidy could practically *see* them walking around, hear their voices as they spoke.

She even found her imagination filling in the words...

With her short lap belt undone, she turned in her seat and found Will standing beside the open-sided cart. He held out a large hand to help her down, and in her excitement Cassidy forgot all the reasons why she shouldn't let him hold on to the hand she slipped into his as he led her down the deserted pseudo-New York street.

After a few steps he asked, 'You want to see inside?'

Nodding, she threw another smile his way.

So Will took them to the nearest open doorway and stepped back, setting her hand free to allow her to go ahead of him. 'Some have a room like this they can dress to be any kind of store they want, but most of the buildings only go back a couple of feet from the frontage.'

Cassidy turned a circle in the empty space, tilting her head back to look up at the skeletal structure of wood and ladders. Her nostrils were filled with the scent of that same wood warmed by the Californian heat outside, and it was all too easy to see why there were so many fire extinguishers around. The danger of fire would always be a worry for a studio. The whole place would go up like a tinderbox, wouldn't it?

'When they dress the room they put in a false ceiling and leave space to hang the lighting. If you look outside you'll see there aren't any door handles or streetlights; they get changed by the props department according to the era of the shoot…'

Drinking in every word, she felt her chest fill with what felt distinctly like joy. It had been such a long time since she'd felt that way. She could have wept with how wonderful everything was. To some it might have seemed false and empty, a charade—but not to her. To her it was a world full of possibilities…

Will's deep voice lowered until it was barely above a whisper, making Cassidy wonder for a moment if he'd even realised he'd spoken out loud. 'Yeah, I had a feeling you'd love this.'

Lowering her chin, she caught her breath when she realised how close he was to her. There was the beginning of a smile in the green of his eyes, and the accompanying warmth she could see seemed to reach out and wrap around her like a blanket on a winter's night. Then his gaze studied each of her eyes in turn, thick lashes flickering.

The intensity forced Cassidy to silently clear her throat before she could speak. 'I do. It's amazing. Thank you for bringing me here.'

Will studied her for another long moment that made her feel as if time stood still. Then he took a breath and looked around, shrugging wide shoulders beneath the pale blue shirt he wore loose over his jeans. 'Sometimes seeing where movies are made can help with the writing process. Anything that can be filmed on a back lot or on a stage saves money on the budget. Studios like that.'

It all came down to business for him, didn't it? He saw everything in terms of the bottom dollar. Another thing that was different. Yes, Cassidy knew it was part of his job—but it was yet another reminder that he wasn't the same Will Ryan she had known. In the last twenty-four hours she had actually convinced herself she'd seen brief glimpses of the old Will she had loved. But every time she thought she saw something in him that might help rebuild the merest shadow of the relationship they once had—and would therefore make it easier to remember how well they could work together—it was as if a switch flipped inside him. Then the Will she didn't know and couldn't read was back.

It was both disconcerting and frustrating. For a second she even wanted to grasp hold of his wide shoulders and shake him, demand that he let out the Will she knew from behind the impenetrable wall he seemed to have built around himself.

'I guess you have to worry more about that kind of stuff these days?'

'I do.' He wandered around the empty room, glancing briefly out through the windows clouded almost opaque with dust. 'It's one thing letting your imagination run riot in a script, but it's another producing something all the way through onto the screen.'

Cassidy nodded, her gaze following him around the room. He was practically prowling. Almost restless, silently alert, his steps taking him in a wide circle around her. His gaze slid unerringly to tangle with hers at regular intervals, and it felt as if he was assessing her, trying to decide what to say and what not to. It felt vaguely predatory to her. But that was ridiculous…

Finding her mouth dry again, she swallowed, and then dampened her lips before asking, 'So tell me what your company does.'

Pushing his hands into his pockets—a move Cassidy noticed he made a lot—Will continued circling her. 'We're responsible for the development and physical production of films and television shows. Sometimes we're directly responsible for the raising of funding for a production—sometimes we do it through an interme- diary. Then we sell the end product to the big studios when it's done.'

'You script some of them yourself?'

'Some, yes.'

'Is it easier to sell your scripts if you can produce them?'

'Not always.' The corners of his mouth tugged wryly.

He was so guarded. Had Hollywood taught him to be that way? she wondered. It was a tough industry, after all. The fact he'd been successful in it meant he'd had to learn to play hard ball at some point. But then Will had always been driven. He'd had a rougher upbringing than most. To go from fostercare kid, handed from home to home, to end up rich and successful in Hollywood was one heck of an achievement. Surely he knew that?

As jealous as she was of his success, in practically every corner of his life in comparison to how very ordinarily hers had turned out, Cassidy was incredibly proud of him. She just wished she could tell him. Not that he wanted or needed to hear it.

'One of our productions is filming on one of the sound stages here. You want to go watch for a while?'

It was enough to put the smile back on her face. 'Can we?'

Will looked amused by her enthusiasm. 'Wouldn't have offered if we couldn't, would I?'

Oh, he could try and make her feel like a child for being so excited by everything he was showing her, but it wasn't going to stop her feeling that way. She rushed to the door and yanked it open to walk into the bright sunshine, jerking her head and grinning at him. 'Hurry up, then. We might miss some of the good stuff.'

An hour later she was sitting on a high folding chair, with her hands over the headphones on her ears, watching the small screen in front of her and listening to the dialogue from the actors mere feet from her. She wasn't even distracted by the fact Will was in a similar chair close beside her—or that every time she glanced at him he was watching her with silent amusement glowing in his eyes. In fact the only thing that took some of the excitement away was when she foolishly allowed reality to seep in around the edges of the experience.

It was a one-off experience for her—and no matter how much joy she felt, it was tainted by the fact it was another fleeting glance of what could have been. Had she been brave enough or selfish enough to leave Ireland behind her, follow the man she loved to California, her life could have been as wrapped up in the world of make-believe as Will's was. With luck, hard work and Will by her side, maybe she'd have made a go of it too. She could have been so happy. Maybe there would even have been a couple of those miniature Wills she kept seeing in her mind's eye running around that beachfront house of his by now...

The thought made her heart twist painfully in her chest.

When the director yelled 'Cut!' she removed the headphones and swallowed away the lump in her throat as she handed them back to the sound engineer. 'Thank you.'

'No problem.' He smiled at her before moving away.

Will's low voice rumbled at her shoulder. 'What's wrong?'

'Nothing's wrong. Thanks again for this, Will—it's been amazing.' She flashed him a smile.

But he could still read her too well, and his eyes narrowed almost imperceptibly. 'Feeling sick again?'

Actually, she'd pretty much forgotten the tail-end of her cold as the day progressed, so she could answer that one with conviction. 'No. I'm feeling much better, as it happens—haven't even needed tablets.'

He continued studying her eyes. 'Then what is it?'

If she lied and said she was tired there was the chance he might suggest they leave—if he didn't see right through her the way he usually did when she lied—and she wasn't ready to leave yet. It wasn't as if she could tell him the truth, was it? How was she supposed to look him in the eye and tell him her active imagination had painted a picture of a life that wasn't hers so vividly that it made her feel the loss of it like a bereavement?

So she avoided his gaze and changed the subject. 'Is this a new show?'

'End of the first season. It's done well in the ratings. Already been renewed.' He waited for her to glance at him again before he added, 'We'll go take a look at the editing department next. Special effects are done somewhere else.'

Cassidy found herself mesmerised by the softness in his deep voice. And her errant tongue couldn't help but ask, 'Why are you doing this?'

Dark brows lifted in question.

'I thought you were mad keen to get the script done.'

He shrugged. 'Thought it might help.'

When he continued looking her straight in the eye, Cassidy had a moment of fear that he might know how much of a fraud she was. Was that what this whole behind-the-scenes day trip was? A way to try and get her creative juices flowing again? In fairness, it was a pretty great plan if that *had* been his aim. But if it had how, exactly, had he known? Had she been so transparent? Had the scenes she'd worked on with him been so dreadful in Hollywood terms? If they had, why hadn't he said so? If he knew what a phoney she was why hadn't he said something? Bringing her all the way across the world to allow her to make a fool of herself when in all probability he could more than likely have just bought her out of the contract...

'You were always as fascinated by this stuff as I was.' He stared into her eyes for another long moment, then looked away, turning his profile to her as he got to his feet. 'Seeing it should keep it real in your mind while we work on the script. And if we can cut a few corners by filming some scenes here instead of on location then we can free up some of the budget for better effects.'

Ah. Right. *Business*. That made more sense to her than him doing it because he knew how much she would love it. It put her mind at ease that he hadn't seen right through her charade. She didn't feel any better, though—it would have been nice if he'd cared enough to do it just because he knew the pleasure she would get from it.

But then Will Ryan had long since ceased to think of

Cassidy in terms of anything remotely resembling the word 'pleasure'—physically or otherwise…

  She nodded firmly and edged off the seat. 'Editing department it is, then.'

CHAPTER FOUR

THEY'D spent most of the day at the studio, so it meant they had to spend the next few days digging in. To Cassidy's amazement it was going pretty well, all things considered.

Will's guided tour had indeed given her an extra dimension of insight to the logistics of each scene they came up with, and—even though she knew he hadn't intended it—it had also got her creative juices flowing. When they started getting words down on paper she felt as if she was getting a part of herself back again. It was exhilarating, and it boosted her self-confidence no end. Heck, she was even starting to have *fun*.

That would be the reason she would cite later for not having seen the danger coming her way before it arrived. Because if she'd been paying more attention...

When they couldn't agree on what should happen at the end of an action scene, Will came up with the idea that they read the lines aloud. Nothing unusual about that, she had thought at the time. It wasn't anything new, after all. When they had worked on the first of Nick Fortune's adventures they'd often acted out a scene before they'd even put words down, and sometimes they'd become so absorbed in the roles they were playing that it had added a dimension to the fictional characters they might never have thought of otherwise.

But back then they'd had a very different relationship. And it never occurred to Cassidy to take that into consideration when they got to their feet with their matching sheets of script in hand, hot from the printer.

Nick and Rachel had got themselves into trouble, and had been arguing about whose fault it was they were in the mess they were. They were minutes away from being tossed off the edge of a cliff by armed terrorists…

"'I suppose you're going to kill us now?" *That's* what you asked them? Why didn't you just offer to shoot us too?' said Will as Nick.

'Oooohhh,' laughed Cassidy as Rachel. 'Believe me if I had a gun right now I'd be more than happy to shoot you!'

She grinned when Will changed his voice to read one of the terrorists' lines. 'Would you two shut up? You've got about five minutes to make your peace.' He threw her an all too brief smile before jerking his chin at her to indicate it was her line.

Cassidy lifted her sheet and tried to find where they were. 'Just make sure *he* goes first. He's the one that got us into this mess.'

'*Me*? I'm not the one who screamed and gave away our position!'

'That spider was the size of Moby Dick!' Cassidy couldn't help but laugh again at the line. She *loved* that line. It was her line; she'd thought of it. She was *back*! What had made her think she couldn't do this again?

Will became Will again. 'Which brings us to the part under debate…'

The original idea had been to have Nick and Rachel fight their way out of the situation by distracting the terrorists with increased arguing. Cassidy had wanted it to be Rachel's idea; funnily enough Will had wanted it to be Nick's. Will suggested Nick should wink at Rachel, to let her know what he was doing. Cassidy said Rachel was too mad at him to play along with anything he came up with.

Suddenly Will looked at her, with a gaze that made her heart jump out of rhythm.

'What?' she asked a little breathlessly.

'I have an idea.' He stepped closer. 'Play along.'

Cassidy turned her head and eyed him with suspicion. 'What are you doing?'

'They get to the edge of the cliff. They're still arguing. Guns at their backs.'

'Uh-huh… And then…?'

Something dangerous shimmered across Will's eyes as he closed the gap between them, his deep voice lowering to a husky-edged rumble. 'Then, just before they're pushed over the edge, Nick asks for a last request for a dying man…'

'And that request would be…?'

Will smiled *that* smile and knocked her on her ear again. 'He asks to kiss Rachel.'

Cassidy's eyes widened. 'He *what*?'

'Just for the record, her face looks exactly like yours does right now…'

Somewhere in the foggy haze of her completely distracted brain Cassidy knew it would ramp up the scene to a new level, but that wasn't what made her heart thunder loudly in her ears and her body temperature rise. *No*. It was the fact that Will was staring down at her with a darkening gaze.

He wasn't seriously going to—?

Thick dark lashes lowered slowly as he took the last step to bring his body within inches of hers. And as she swayed a little on her feet he angled his head, his gaze lowering to focus on her mouth. Oh, God. *He was*. But why? He couldn't—

Cassidy's lips reached for his of their own volition when he was less than an inch away, like a flower lifting towards the sun. His mouth was full and firm and hotter than she remembered from the hundreds of times she'd kissed him before, but no less familiar. When his large hands framed her face, she took a deep breath through her nose. When he leaned into her she exhaled against his lips, her heavy eyelids closing...

If anyone had told her a month ago that some time in the very near future Will Ryan would be kissing her again, and she would be feeling it in every cell in her body, she'd have laughed out loud at the ridiculousness of the notion. But he was—and she did.

It was surreal. And at the same time it was like coming home.

Long fingers slid down her cheeks, around her neck and into her hair. The taste of him was on her lips and the heady scent of clean laundry and pure Will was surrounding her. Cassidy forgot about the script, forgot about the fact they were playing the part of Nick and Rachel, forgot about the danger in what they were doing. She forgot all those things.

Instead she dropped her sheet of paper and reached for handfuls of the shirt above his lean waist, while he slipped a hand up to cradle the back of her head, his fingers threading into her hair as Cassidy drowned in the sensations flooding her body.

She'd missed kissing him. *How she'd missed it.* It was as if her body had been asleep like Snow White's, and only now, with the right man, was she being kissed back into life. But then no one had ever kissed her like Will kissed her. He could make the world tilt on its axis beneath her feet. *Always.* From the very first time he'd kissed her. He'd caught her similarly off-guard as they'd walked over the O'Connell Street Bridge in Dublin, after taking photographs of possible locations for a short film they'd been working on for their class. With no warning he had taken her hand, tugged her to him and kissed her. *Because he had to*, he had told her afterwards. As if it had been as vital to him as breathing or drinking water, or any of the other things a person had to do to survive…

When he slowly drew his lips from hers, her mouth followed his back for the inch she'd closed, her eyes opening wide and searching his with a combination of wonder and fear.

After a brief moment of studying her with a dark unreadable gaze, Will rested his cheek against hers, whispering into her ear in a husky voice, 'Then Nick says, "You take the one on the left".'

Cassidy's heart plummeted to the soles of her feet.

Will released her and stepped back, turning abruptly and informing her in a flat, businesslike voice, 'That works better. So, we'll add that in and jump straight to the fight and the chase scene…'

'Right.' Cassidy nodded dumbly while she tried to get her breathing under control. The script. Nick and Rachel. Not Will and Cassidy. That was what the kiss had been about. He hadn't kissed her because he'd wanted to. He'd just forgotten they didn't have the same relationship now they'd had before when they would have played out similar Nick and Rachel scenes—*apparently*.

Bending down to retrieve the sheets of paper on the floor, she took a deep breath and puffed out her cheeks as she exhaled. She could only pray he wasn't planning on acting out the love scene they had planned for Scene Three…

She didn't think she could survive Will Ryan breaking her heart twice in one lifetime. She wasn't entirely sure she'd got over the first time.

The kiss changed things. At least it did for Cassidy. She tried not to let it, but she couldn't stop it—partly because she couldn't seem to get it out of her head…

What she needed to do was focus on what they were doing. Heck, at this point she would even take a stab at re-building some kind of platonic friendship with Will. After all, she had to work across a desk from him every day. How was she supposed to do any of those things if every time she looked at him she was thinking about how it had felt to be kissed by him and to kiss him back? Why was she so obsessed by it anyway? It wasn't as if she'd kissed him back because she'd wanted to—at least she told herself it wasn't. She'd been playing a part, the same way he had, thinking on her feet, reacting to what he'd done—that was all. It didn't *mean* anything.

Darn it, he was looking at her again. She could *feel it*. Every time he did it the hair on the back of her neck tingled.

'Stir crazy?'

She kept pacing around the room, the same way she had for most of the two days since they'd kissed. 'I'm fine.'

'Well, I'm not,' his voice rumbled back. 'All that pacing is making *me* crazy.' Will sighed heavily. 'You're not used to sharing space with someone these days, are you? I never pictured you as that much of a loner…'

Cassidy stopped dead in her tracks and angled her head. 'Excuse me?'

'Lived with someone else after me, did you?'

Her jaw dropped. What business was it of his who she had or hadn't lived with? She could have lived with twenty men. Not that she *had* lived with anyone else, barring the time she'd lived in her father's house while he was ill. But that wasn't the point.

A few times over the years she'd considered advertising for a flatmate, but by then she'd got used to having her own space. Living on her own, she didn't have to worry about someone else's opinions on things like what TV channel to watch, or how loud she could play music, or any of a dozen other compromises a person made when they shared living space.

'Compromises…'

Cassidy frowned when he said the very thing she'd just thought—as if he'd somehow stepped inside her head. 'What?'

'I said living with someone involves compromises.'

'It does.' She nodded. 'And forced intimacy…'

'Shared responsibilities…'

When he looked up at her she turned away and began pacing again, the words quietly slipping off the tip of her tongue. 'Never being alone.'

She frowned sideways at him when she said it, confusion clouding her vision as he studied her with a curious expression that almost said he suspected why she'd been so uneasy with him of late. She hoped he didn't! But while he continued staring at her there was an inexplicably heavy tension in the room.

Her chin lifted. 'Okay. Fine. You're right—all are things I suck royally at. Barring the last one. I excel at being alone these days—it's what I do best.'

'Cass…' He kept his voice low. 'Living with someone is nothing like what we're doing now. You know that. And being alone isn't—'

'Of course it's nothing like this. This is artificial. And temporary.' Cassidy tried to figure out why that felt so bad and couldn't seem to find an answer. Maybe being alone for so long had affected her more than she'd realized? She started pacing again. 'This isn't sharing space. It's temporary. A charade.'

'A charade?' he repeated dryly.

She glanced sideways at him again as she changed direction. 'Oh, come on. It's miraculous enough that we've managed to work together this last while…'

'We shared space before and it was never this much of a problem…' Will reached for his mug and frowned when he discovered it was empty. 'You want coffee?'

He didn't wait for an answer, reaching across the large desk for her empty mug and pushing his squeaky chair back. 'I don't think this has anything to do with sharing space with me. I think trying to keep me at arm's length is starting to take its toll on you.'

When he left the room her feet immediately followed him. 'And what exactly is *that* supposed to mean?'

'I think you know what it means.'

How dared he assume he knew her every thought? Just because nine times out of ten he was in the ballpark area, it didn't mean he could read her damn mind.

She followed him across the living room. 'So if I'm not throwing myself at you it means I'm fighting some inner battle, does it? How do you get that head of yours through doors?'

Setting their mugs down on the breakfast bar, Will went about refilling the coffee-maker, replacing the filter and spooning in coffee granules. 'Doesn't have anything to do with throwing yourself at me. You're determined not to allow yourself to even be friends with me again. It's childish, frankly. We're both adults.'

Placing her hands on her hips, she stopped dead at one end of the breakfast bar, speechless.

With the coffee set to percolate, Will turned around, leaning nonchalantly against the counter-top on the opposite side of the kitchen from her and calmly folding his arms across the studio logo on his T-shirt. 'You're different. The Cass I met in the Beverly Wilshire just over a week ago isn't the girl I knew in Dublin. The girl I knew in Dublin was open-minded and honest to the point of bluntness, and she would never have let something brood in her the way you have since you got here. So let's just clear the air and get it over with, shall we?'

Cassidy opened her mouth to tell him to go straight to—

But he looked her in the eye and knocked the air out of her lungs by saying, 'You blame me for our break-up, don't you?'

He wasn't done, either. Not content with opening the can of worms, he then twisted the knife she felt she had in her chest by adding, 'Maybe you should just take a minute and remember who it was that did the breaking up before I left…'

The sharp gasp of air hurt her already raw throat.

Then a muted doorbell sounded, and the door at the top of the stairs was flung open. 'Hello? Anybody home? Time to put down the keyboard!'

Cassidy had a brief glimpse of the frown on Will's face before she snapped her head around to watch with wide eyes as Angelique appeared. If it wasn't surprise enough finding out that the woman had a key to Will's house, there was then a thundering of footsteps and a small blonde-haired ball of energy ran down the stairs, across the wooden floor, and launched itself into Will's waiting arms.

'Uncle Will!'

Uncle Will? Cassidy couldn't help it; her jaw dropped. Not just at the sight of the little girl throwing her small arms around the column of his neck. What really amazed her was Will's expression as he held her. He was transformed. Gone was the intense, unreadable, pain-in-the-rear Will, and in his place was a man who looked as if he'd just shed five years. Light danced in his eyes, he grinned broadly, and there was the sound of deep, rumbling, happy laughter before he made an exaggerated groan and leaned his head back to look down at her.

'Hey, munchkin.'

'We brought a picnic!'

'Did you, now?' He lifted his dark brows as he looked in Angelique's direction, 'Did I know we were having a picnic?'

'It's a surprise, silly!' the little girl informed him.

'Indeed it is,' he answered dryly.

Angelique had made it to Cassidy's side. 'This is what

happens when you two stand me up for dinner. Script or no script, you still have to eat.'

Will looked up as he bent to set the child on her feet. 'We have managed to feed ourselves on our own. Ever hear of a little thing called a phone, Angie?'

'Ah, but if we'd phoned ahead it wouldn't be a sur- prise, would it?'

'Remind me to ask for my key back some time.'

Cassidy was rapidly putting two and two together. She even found her gaze sliding across to the little girl who was tugging on Will's jeans to see if she could see any simi- larities between them. Having had such vivid images of miniature Wills in her mind since she'd arrived in his gorgeous house, she felt the ragged edges of her heart grate painfully at the thought of finding any. She didn't *want* Will to have any children she might be forced to look at. The thought of him having them with any woman who wasn't her was apparently painful enough.

Which made no sense whatsoever, considering how much she currently disliked him and how close they had been to a major argument not five minutes earlier.

'Uncle Will?'

He hunched down to look the little girl in the eye; the thoughtfulness of the simple act made Cassidy's heart hurt all over again. 'Yes, munchkin, what can I do for you?'

'The picnic's for the beach.'

'Is it indeed?'

She nodded enthusiastically. 'And I brought my swim- suit and my bodyboard.'

'Ah.' Will pursed his mouth into a thin line and frowned almost comically at her, before taking a deep breath through his nose. 'We'd better go check the sea is still there, then, hadn't we?'

The little girl giggled, and Cassidy found herself smiling at them as Angelique linked their arms at the elbow and lowered her voice conspiratorially. 'Sometimes I wonder who has who wrapped around their little finger. I hope you've brought a bikini with you?'

The thought of publicly displaying her body on a Malibu beach next to the goddess that was Angelique Warden made Cassidy want to curl up in a ball and die. That was not happening in this lifetime. Not that she owned a bikini to begin with, but still...

'Will could give you a surfing lesson while he's helping Lily bodyboard.'

Cassidy's gaze shifted sharply and crashed into Will's as he stood to his full height. Then her troublesome imagination revisited the image she'd had of him emerging from the surf and she swallowed hard. For a moment she even thought she could hear herself making a gulping noise.

Thick lashes blinked while he stared at her. The intensity returning to his gaze was even fiercer than before. Oh, please, *please* don't let now be one of the times when he can read my mind, she silently pleaded. There was only so much humiliation she could take.

Then he nodded. 'You'll need sunscreen. Beach towels are in the laundry room. Angie knows where everything is.'

Before Cassidy could protest, he turned his attention to Lily. 'Right, then. While Cass and I get changed, you and your mom can go get this picnic we've been promised. Are there cookies?'

'*Duh*, Uncle Will.'

* * *

Despite many, many, *many* carefully worded protests, Cassidy found herself on the beach—thankfully in a swimsuit rather than a bikini. Even that was covered by a thigh-length light shirt. Smothered in the highest factor sunscreen she'd packed, she also had the large-brimmed straw hat Angelique had left behind on her last visit to Will's house on her head. She had the prerequisite sunglasses on, and had bent one knee as artfully as she could manage as she sat on the large blanket beside the bikini-clad Angelique. If people squinted Cassidy reckoned they might look like nineteen-fifties movie star next to modern-day goddess. Hopefully. After all, women had been adored for their hourglass figures back then—which meant, as always, her timing was severely off. Not that it made her feel any more comfortable in her own skin.

Watching Will playing in the surf with Lily was the worst form of water torture she'd ever been submitted to. It was just plain *wrong* to be drooling at the sight of him in long swim shorts—bare chest, toned, tanned, gorgeous enough to die for—while he played with a small child. Especially if he was that small child's father, and she was sitting chatting to the woman he'd made that child with. Cassidy had never had a worse case of the green-eyed monster in all her life.

'Lily adores him.' Angelique was smiling at them when Cassidy looked her way. 'He'll make a great father some day.'

Cassidy exhaled with relief as quietly as she could manage it. 'She's gorgeous.'

'Obviously I think so. But then I'm a tad biased. Do you have kids, Cass?'

'Thirty of them.' She smiled at Angelique's expression. 'I'm a schoolteacher.'

'Ahh. You scared me for a minute.'

Despite a lingering modicum of jealousy over her relationship with Will, Cassidy found herself warming to Angie. She wasn't at all the way the tabloids portrayed her. And seeing her obvious love for her daughter humanised her.

Turning onto her stomach, Angie swung her feet back and forth in the air and studied Cassidy from behind her sunglasses. 'Did you and Will ever talk about having kids when you were together?'

It was a very personal question, but by asking it she'd already shown she knew there had been more to their relationship than being scriptwriting duo Ryan and Malone. The thing was, talking about their relationship with someone who might well be in, or have been in, a similar relationship with Will made Cassidy uncomfortable.

So she sought a simple answer. 'We were young.'

The fact she'd said it with a shrug of her shoulders didn't seem to fool Angie. 'Ever since I've known Will he's been reluctant to talk about you. It took us to get him drunk one night before he would even talk about growing up in Ireland…'

He'd talked about his childhood? Wow. Cassidy wondered if Angie knew what a big deal that was for Will. She'd been dating him for nearly a year before she'd got the full story— though in fairness she hadn't had to get him drunk.

But her brain had latched onto one seemingly insignificant word. *'Us?'*

Angie examined the perfectly manicured fingernails on one hand. 'Lily's father—my on-again off-again partner Eric—is one of Will's best friends. It's how I got to know Will. And why he's Lily's godfather.'

Immediately Cassidy's gaze sought them out again in the sea. Will was swinging the little girl round and round in circles, while she squealed in delight and he grinned boyishly at her. 'Oh.'

She'd got that one completely wrong, then, hadn't she?

There was a chuckle of laughter. 'Yes, I wondered if you'd thought that. You're delightfully easy to read, aren't you? I can't tell you how refreshing that is in Hollywood.'

Heat built on Cassidy's cheeks that had absolutely nothing to do with the sun.

'Can I ask you a question, Cass?'

A sense of dread made her cringe as she looked down at the woman she had a sneaking suspicion was about to ask the one question she didn't want to answer. 'Depends on what it is.'

Angelique smiled. 'I've wondered why Will didn't bring you with him.'

'When he moved here from Ireland?'

'Yes. You were quite the writing team, on top of the re-lationship you had.'

Okay, not the question she'd been waiting for. Maybe that was why she answered it honestly, her chin dropping and her voice lowering even though there wasn't any chance he could hear her from where he was. 'I couldn't leave.'

'So he did ask?'

'Yes.' It was a simplistic answer to a situation that had been very complicated.

There was a moment of silence, then, 'Do you regret it?'

Cassidy smiled sadly. 'That's not an easy one to answer. It's not a case of regretting; it's more of a case of what was right and what was wrong at the time, and what was meant to be and what wasn't. And I have *no idea* why I'm telling you this…'

'Maybe you need a friend?' Angelique waited until Cassidy looked at her, and then she nodded sharply and beamed. 'I've decided I like you, Cass. I think we'll be great friends. You don't treat me like a movie star, and that's a huge bonus.'

Cassidy lowered her voice to a conspiratorial whisper. 'You *are* a movie star.'

Angie lowered her voice to a similar level, 'Shh. Somebody might hear you.'

They were laughing when the sun was suddenly blocked out, forcing Cassidy to shade her eyes with a hand as she looked up at the dark silhouette surrounded by bright light.

'Ready for your surfing lesson?'

CHAPTER FIVE

'I DON'T actually want a surfing lesson. Honestly.'

'Don't knock it till you've tried it.' Will turned round and took the two steps required to get to where she'd been dragging her heels. Reaching out, he captured her wrist in long fingers and tugged her along behind him. 'You might like it.'

'I'll sink like a whale,' she grumbled.

'Whales don't sink; they swim. So will you.' He threw a frown over his shoulder as he continued tugging her along the sand, 'Stop being paranoid about your weight, Cass. Women are supposed to curve. I'm sick to death of being surrounded by stick-thin women counting the calories in a bottle of water.'

Trying to free her wrist was getting her nowhere. 'Bullying me again, Ryan?'

'Nope. Forcing you to have a good time. It's for your own good. You seem to have forgotten how.'

'Said by the man who doesn't have time to go surfing, having bought a house by the ocean for that very purpose? I think you'll find that falls into the category of *I will when you will*,' she retorted.

He stopped so suddenly she careened into the wall of

his back, and grunted in a very unladylike manner before scowling up at his face.

The sight of his face leaning closer to hers made her eyes widen. That was before he lowered his voice and rumbled a meaningful, 'Oh, I know how to have *fun*, Cass. Don't you worry…'

Judging by the glint in his eyes, he wasn't talking about surfing fun either.

Standing back a little, he frowned at her body. 'That's got to go.'

When he released her wrist, she lifted both hands to grip hold of her shirt as if he might try to remove it at any second. 'The shirt *stays*.'

Will folded his arms across the sculpted chest she was trying very hard not to look at. 'You *do* know it's going to be transparent in the water, don't you?'

Actually, that thought hadn't occurred to her. But now he'd pointed it out she was even less likely to participate in a surfing lesson than she had been sixty seconds ago…

She started backing away. 'Well, I don't know about you, but I'm famished. I've heard a rumour there's a picnic on the go, so I think we should just—'

There was a short chuckle of deep male laughter, and then he leaned over and captured her wrist again, shaking his head as he tugged her forward. 'Down on your stomach on the board…'

Huh? Her gaze dropped and discovered a surfboard on the sand. She scowled at his words. 'On my stomach? On the board?'

He ducked down a little to get her attention, his nose mere inches from hers. 'Surfing lesson—remember?'

'I thought it would be in the water.' How was she supposed to think straight when he was so close?

Will's gaze dropped briefly to her mouth when she dampened her lips, then lifted to tangle with hers for equally as brief a moment before he leaned back and looked down at the board. 'Basics on dry land. *Then* we go in the water.'

Well, how was she supposed to know that? Okay, on her stomach—with Will standing over her, looking down at her rear. Cassidy silently prayed for a tidal wave…

'Why am I getting on my stomach?'

'Because that's what you do to paddle the board out far enough to catch an incoming wave…'

Right. Except that statement presupposed she actually *wanted* to catch a wave—which frankly she didn't. Waves shouldn't be caught. Cassidy believed they should be allowed to roam the earth in freedom, with all their other wave friends. She might even start a campaign of some kind: *Save the Wave*. Catchy, she thought.

She sighed heavily, focused her mind on another method of stalling Will, and came up with, 'Maybe you should demonstrate first?'

With a shake of his head that indicated he was fully aware of what she was doing, Will dropped onto the board, leaving her staring down at him in the same way she'd feared he would stare at her. Somehow she had the feeling her view was much better than his would be. Then he started to move his arms, and she became fascinated with the play of muscles on his tanned back. Was he working out nowadays? She didn't remember him being so…*toned*…

'Paddle evenly with both arms, and then turn and watch

for a wave. Try to time it so you jump to your feet as it hits your board.' He demonstrated by jumping lithely to his feet and reaching his arms out to his sides for balance. 'Then use your feet to steer the board. If you shift your weight to your toes you'll go one way; rock back onto your heels and you go the other.'

He made it sound so easy. But his description of brain surgery would probably consist of *Pop skull open, move jelly stuff around and put lid back on*. Whereas Cassidy suspected *her* version of surfing would involve less of the standing up and more of the getting wet and spluttering as she tried to get salt water out of her lungs.

'Your turn.' Will stepped off the board and quirked his brows when she hesitated, his voice lowering and his eyes sparkling. '*Chicken*. Whatever happened to the hunger to learn and the spirit of adventure you used to have?'

Cassidy threw another scowl at him, pursed her lips and lowered herself cautiously onto the board. 'I really do hate you, you know.'

'No, you don't.' He hunched down beside her.

When she was on her stomach, she looked up at him in time to see his gaze rise from studying her body. It made her laugh. 'Oh, yes, I do.'

The first time she attempted jumping up to her feet she fell over, but managed to get a hand on the hot sand to help right herself. Will encouraged her with a low, 'Try again.'

The second time she fell on her rear, and frowned hard at his obvious amusement. He cleared his throat and held out a hand to help her up. 'Again.'

Cassidy growled at him. 'When does it start to be fun, exactly?'

The third time was the charm. She not only fell over, she fell on Will, and toppled him backwards onto the sand, creating a tangle of legs and forcing him to wrap her body in his arms. Yup—her run of incredible luck had continued. Because when she puffed air at the loose strand of hair that had got in her eyes and looked down her face was inches away from his. And he was smiling one of *those* smiles.

Someone, somewhere really had it in for her.

The heat from his bare chest seeped through the thin material of her shirt and made every cell of her body unbearably aware of where she was fitted against him. It was like being set on fire. She felt the lack of oxygen to her brain making her dizzy, felt the ache of physical awareness so keenly it almost snapped her in two. Then one large hand lifted, and impossibly gentle fingertips brushed her hair back and tucked the strand behind her ear.

Cassidy felt her heart beating so hard against her sensitised breasts that she was certain Will must feel the erratic rhythm too. She needed to say something funny to break the tension—needed to move as far away from him as possible before he realised how damn turned on she was—needed—

She saw his throat convulse before he took a deep breath that crushed her breasts tighter to the wall of his chest. 'We should try again.'

What? Her eyes widened at the words. He couldn't possibly mean—

Will studied her eyes, then rolled her to the side. 'You need to pick a point in front of you to focus on as you jump onto your feet. That'll make it easier to balance…'

Struggling awkwardly to her feet while she felt her cheeks burning, Cassidy avoided his gaze and frowned at her foolishness—or her wishful thinking, or whatever it was that had made her heart leap the way it had. 'If I can't do this on dry land I don't see how I stand a bat's chance of doing it on moving water.'

While she bent over to swipe the sand off her legs, Will's deep voice sounded above her head. 'Don't give up so easy, Cass. Some things are worth the effort.'

Her gaze shot up to tangle with his and he shrugged. 'You love the ocean. Always did. Makes sense that anything that allows you to appreciate it more you'll end up enjoying.'

Several hours later she discovered he was right. The fact he'd been just the right degree of persuasive, determined and patient at varying stages to get her to that point had not gone unnoticed either. Any more than she'd failed to notice when he saw his theory on the transparency of her shirt when wet had been right too.

It was her last attempt. She managed to stay upright long enough to ride the wave for several feet, and the exhilaration of achievement burst forth from her lips in joyous laughter at the same time as Will let out a victory yell. When she inevitably fell off and surfaced from the water, lifting her hands to smooth her wet hair back from her face as she grinned like an idiot, she looked up—and her grin faltered. He had hold of the board as he waded towards her, waist deep in water the same way she was. But then he lifted his chin, his gaze travelling across the foaming surface and sliding up her body oh-so-very-slowly.

When he looked into her eyes the heat she could see both robbed her of her ability to breathe and slammed into her midriff with such force that the next wave almost made her lose her footing in the shifting sands.

For the longest time they stared at each other. The ebb and flow of the tide dragging her abdomen back and forth was all too evocative, considering the ferocity of her physical desire, and eliciting a low moan from the base of her throat that the wind thankfully dragged away. Then Will frowned—hard—turning his head and looking out to sea so that Cassidy caught sight of a muscle moving in his clenched jaw.

Almost in slow motion she saw him exerting control over himself. It was heartbreaking. Especially considering the fact that she was faced with the very image of him she'd conjured in her imagination when he had first told her he surfed. Standing there, with silvery rivulets of water running off his body, shining silvery in the bright sunshine, droplets of the same shimmering water falling from wet tendrils of the dark hair that clung to his forehead and the column of his neck. *He was glorious.* More than that, even. He was the most sensationally sexy man she had ever laid eyes on. And she had never wanted him as much as she did at that moment—while he'd taken a deep breath and got his self-control back in the blink of an eye.

When he looked at her again the small smile on his full mouth didn't make it all the way up into his eyes. 'Told you you'd get it. Well done.'

But Cassidy couldn't let it go that easily. And the very fact he had so obviously been affected by her gave her enough of a subliminal confidence boost to take a step towards him. 'Will—'

His eyes narrowed at the husky edge of her voice. 'I'm going to catch a few waves of my own. Be back in a while.'

With that he turned away, got on the board, paddled further out to sea—and the moment was gone. He'd made it plain that whatever moment of remembered desire from the past he'd just experienced could be dismissed in a heart-beat. Men were supposed to think about sex at ridiculously regular intervals, so they said. Cassidy was merely a woman in the nearest equivalent of a wet T-shirt. She got that.

But the rejection hurt. It hurt *bad.*

Setting a sheet of the first draft of their script to one side after she'd proofread it, Cassidy reached for another. Even though they worked in silence for the following fifteen minutes, she could still feel him studying her. He'd been doing it for days. And it was getting to her big-time.

'What, Will?'

'I'm just thinking of going to the kitchen to get a knife.'

'To do what?' She didn't look at him. He might have been studying her like some kind of bug under a micro-scope, but since the beach she'd been able to look at him for no longer than a few seconds before she had to avert her gaze. Apparently his rejection still hurt. And looking at him made it worse.

'To cut the atmosphere in this room...'

She sighed heavily. 'Will—'

'Right.' He pushed to his feet and lifted the sheets from her hand, setting them to one side. Then he grabbed hold of her hands and tugged. 'Time for a change of scenery. And lunch.'

It was beginning to feel as if she'd been trapped in the house with Will for years on end. People didn't get jail sen-tences as long. Every hour felt as if it was dragging. Plus, if Will kept feeding her the way he was she was going to go home weighing more than when she'd arrived.

The second she was on her feet he let go of her hands, turned, and headed into the next room. Cassidy automatically fell into step behind him, somehow unable to drag her disobedient gaze from the errant curls of dark hair brushing the collar of his cream shirt. It was easier looking at him when he didn't know she was, she supposed…

'We'll eat on the deck,' he announced as he glanced over his shoulder. 'The ocean is supposed to have a calming effect.'

Cass shook her head at his dry wit as they moved into the kitchen. 'You want me to take anything out?'

'Juice and glasses would be good.'

She opened a cupboard for glasses and the fridge for juice, feeling a pang of sadness at how they moved around each other as if they'd been doing it for years. It was like a choreographed dance. He reached an arm up to the cupboard door; she ducked under it. She turned for the fridge; he circled around her in one fluent step. She opened the refrigerator door to put away the juice; he reached inside for mayo and ham before he closed it again…

Cassidy had watched her parents doing a similar dance hundreds of times over the years during her childhood, and had never appreciated how much it demonstrated their ease with each other. But then they'd had decades to learn the moves; Cassidy and Will hadn't had all that long even when they were together.

Without thinking she casually handed him a chopping board on her way to opening the sliding doors. When he looked sideways at her, he frowned for a second before taking it.

'It's always beautiful out here,' she said from the doorway.

'I know,' Will answered, with a smile in his deep voice.

Stepping on to the deck, she set the glasses down on a small table and then moved towards the railing, where she breathed deep and smiled. It was the kind of place she would have allowed herself to relax and just 'be', under better circumstances. She wondered if Will ever felt that way. Pleasure in the simple things had never been the young Will's thing—not that he hadn't appreciated them; he'd just always been ambitious for more. But Cassidy had learned how precious and fragile life could be. It was important to take pleasure in the simple things, she felt.

But, looking at the ocean, she found her thoughts wandering inevitably to the same things. For the hundredth time since it had happened she found herself revisiting what had happened the day he'd taught her to surf—which in turn led her to revisiting the kiss during their 'rehearsal'. She had no idea why she was so obsessed by that kiss. Okay, admittedly the mature version of Will was oh-so-sexy—she would have to be blind not to have noticed. Under tall, dark and handsome in the dictionary it probably said *see Will Ryan.*

The sound of a plate being set on the table behind her gave her enough warning to get her thoughts under control before he appeared in her peripheral vision. Then they stood there for a while, side-by-side in silence, before Cassidy chanced a sideways glance at him just as Will turned his head to look at her.

He smiled a more genuine smile than he had in days, and she felt another shiver of awareness as he asked in his deliciously deep voice, 'Better?'

'I shook the cold a week ago.'

'That wasn't what I meant.'

Yes, she knew it wasn't what he'd meant. Since stalling never seemed to work with him any better than lying did, she took a deep breath and admitted, 'I'm sorry. I guess being cooped up in that room is starting to get to me…'

Will nodded his head, as if he'd already known the answer, his gaze shifting back to the ocean. After a few moments he said, 'Thank you.'

'For what?'

Turning around, he reached out and lifted a glass before smiling at her with a light sparkling in the green of his eyes. 'For helping with lunch.'

Cass smiled back at him. *Liar.* But she didn't call him on it; she appreciated that he hadn't pushed her any further on why she was feeling the way she was. Apparently a little honesty really did go a long way. Anyway, she had a sneaking suspicion he already knew, and was letting her off the hook by not saying it out loud. She should really thank him in return for that. But she didn't, because that would be bringing it up all over again. Instead she turned away from the railing and sat down in one of the comfortably padded wicker chairs on the deck, reaching for a sandwich as Will did the same and sank into a matching chair beside her.

They managed a whole ten minutes of companionable silence, but then he casually ruined it by asking, 'So… you want to tell me what else has been bugging you?'

The half-eaten sandwich froze halfway to her mouth, her appetite waning. Then she took a deep breath and went right ahead and took a bite, filling one side of her cheek as she chewed.

'Okay, then.' Will lifted another sandwich. 'I'll just ask

every half hour from here on in until you yell it at me in the middle of an argument. That usually works.'

Then he glanced at her from the corner of his eye and had the gall to add a wink. She forced herself to speak. 'Still got that pitbull quality to your personality, don't you?'

'Mmm-hmm.' He took a large bite of sandwich and grinned at her as he chewed.

'That wasn't actually meant as a compliment…'

He spoke with the food still in his mouth. 'I prefer to think of it as a dogged determination to get to the root of an issue before it becomes a bigger problem than it needs to be.' Ridiculously thick lashes brushed against his skin a couple of times while he considered her and swallowed his food. 'If my memory serves right—letting you work things through in your head for too long before you talk about them does that.'

'I've been stuck under a roof with someone I can barely hold a conversation with for two weeks. How is that *not* supposed to get to me? Maybe I have a *right* to be moody for a while under those circumstances?'

'No, you don't. Not if talking about it is all it takes to fix it.' He frowned, 'Who *likes* being moody anyway?'

Shrugging her shoulders, Cassidy focused her attention on her sandwich, mumbling under her breath, 'In my experience cute guys who think it adds to their feeble attempts at seeming mysterious…'

There was a very noticeable silence that drew her gaze back to his face, where a stunned expression was warring with amusement. She scowled at him. 'What now?'

'You think I'm *cute*?'

'I didn't say that.' Well, not on purpose she hadn't.

'It's okay. I'm fine with you thinking I'm cute. Though I should probably tell you it has a slightly different meaning over here than it does in Ireland…'

'I know what it means over here, and for the record it's not all that different to what it means back home. And I *don't* think that about you.'

Very visibly having to control his smile, Will leaned back and nodded. 'See, I was going to tell you what I really think is making you feel cooped up…and how I feel about the same thing… But now…? Now I think I'm just going to let you come to your own conclusions. That way I get to be both cute *and* mysterious…'

'That's not what I—' She fought the need to throw her sandwich at him as she felt heat rising on her neck. 'Don't edit my lines outside the office, Ryan.'

'You know,' he sighed dramatically, and let loose a killer one of *those* smiles, 'suddenly I'm in a much better mood than I was twenty minutes ago.'

Will had the gall to chuckle, looking at her from the corner of his sparkling eyes. Darn it. He was gloating, wasn't he? What had happened to the supposedly professional relationship they'd agreed to have? Flirting with her, using a combination of random winks, sparkling eyes and *that* smile, could hardly be considered *professional*.

Cassidy felt distinctly as if she was constantly waging a battle of some kind with him and…heaven help her…he was *winning*.

He was showing her that he could read her better than anyone ever had—get under her skin and bug her more than anyone ever had—get her hormones to scatter all rational thought to the wind and make her laugh when she really didn't want to by lifting his eyebrows ridiculously at her like he currently was…

With a shake of her head she dragged her gaze away from him, to look for some of the peace the ocean had briefly brought her way. 'You are still the most annoying man on the planet, you know.'

'Ahh…but I'm also *cute*.' He inhaled deeply through his nose, smug satisfaction oozing from the rumble of his voice. 'And *mysterious*…'

When she glanced sideways she saw him take another bite of his sandwich. Instead of saying anything smart in return she did the same thing. They sat for another ten minutes in what could almost have been misconstrued as a companionable silence, eating and looking out over the ocean. It was nice. Under further scrutiny Cassidy realised to her complete and utter astonishment it was better than nice. She almost felt…*content*…and it had been a long time since she'd felt that way…

'Do you think she'll ever forgive him?' Will asked.

Cassidy turned her head to look at his face. 'Rachel?'

He nodded, studying her eyes with the silent intensity she was now almost used to. 'She can be pretty bloody-minded when she digs her heels in.'

Cassidy shrugged one shoulder. 'It's self-preservation. Look where being up-front with him got her last time.'

'She knew how Nick felt about her.'

'No. She *thought* she knew how Nick felt about her. Then she convinced herself she was wrong…' A memory from real life wrapped itself around Cassidy's memories of their last script, making her turn her gaze away and frown at the ocean. 'The last argument they had was pretty heated.'

'Lots of things can get said in the heat of an argument that might not have been meant the way they sounded…'

'They can.'

'Maybe we should have them talk it through?'

Cassidy grimaced, then looked sideways at him. 'I think Rachel would rather have needles poked in her eyes.'

'So would Nick. *Hot ones.*'

It made her smile. 'They both need a smack upside the head.'

To her amazement, Will smiled back. 'That would make for a short script.'

'True.'

Dark lashes flickered as he searched her eyes, then Will nodded firmly—just the once—as if he'd made some kind of momentous decision. Swiping a palm against his thigh, he reached his large hand towards her. 'Will Ryan.'

Cassidy arched a brow, her smile still in place. 'What are you doing, you idiot?'

'Starting over.' He jerked his chin at his hand. 'The idea is that you now put your hand in mine and introduce yourself the way I just did. Give it a try. Take a deep breath if you need to. Go on. You can do it.'

'Uh-huh.' The smile grew. 'Patronising me is really going to help your cause.'

Will shook his head. 'Count to ten and swallow down the sarcasm. Otherwise it's going to get to the point where—when we're done with the script—only one of us is coming out of that room alive…'

'You were the one who suggested getting a knife.'

'*Malone.* Don't make me turn on the charm.'

It wasn't an empty threat. If Cassidy hadn't known that

from experience she'd have known it from the way his eyes darkened several shades and his voice lowered an octave to a deep grumble that spoke of tangled sheets and early morning pillow talk. The thought made her smile falter.

Dropping her chin so she could study his outstretched hand with caution, she weighed up the danger of keeping her distance versus taking a chance and ending up friends with him again without her heart wanting more. It was risky.

Long fingers waggled in the air between them, and his voice lowered another octave, sending a shimmer of sensual feminine awareness of nearby hot male across her body. 'Come on, Cass…'

She wondered how he managed to sound like tempta-tion itself—and scary at the same time. Did he even know he was doing it? Or how dangerous a decision it was? Because, despite the intimation, they had never actually been 'friends' at any point of their relationship—there had always been something more.

Taking a deep breath, she swallowed hard and lifted her arm, her hand hesitating mere inches from his. It was Will who closed the gap this time, circling his fingers around hers and holding on—allowing the warmth of his touch to seep through her skin and travel into her veins, where it rushed up her arm towards her racing heart. He clasped more firmly and shook their joined hands up and down.

Then he repeated, in a voice laced with determination, 'Will Ryan. Known to be the most annoying man on the planet at times. Tendency towards occasional arrogance that I'm never going to learn to control. Strange obsession with peanut butter and jelly sandwiches at two in the morning…'

Cassidy smiled as her gaze travelled up his arm, past the

lock of errantly curled hair below his ear to the sparkling green of his eyes. Then she shook her head and swallowed down the need to giggle like a shy schoolgirl. 'Cassidy Malone. Known to be the woman with a natural knack for public humiliation. Tendency to over-think things to the point of complete randomness. Strong belief that peanut butter and jelly anywhere in the vicinity of a slice of bread is just *wrong*…'

'Hello, Cassidy Malone—can I call you Cass?'

'Somehow I doubt I'll be able to stop you.'

Will smiled *that* smile, then cocked his head as he ran the pad of his thumb back and forth over her knuckles. 'We could use this for Nick and Rachel, you know…'

Cassidy rolled her eyes and attempted to quietly extricate her hand from his. 'Just no escaping those two, is there?'

'You want to?' He held onto her hand.

'Do I want to what?'

'Escape them for a while?' The thumb kept brushing over her skin, distracting her from looking away from his mesmerising eyes.

It meant it took a second or two longer than normal for her to focus on what he'd said. 'Will, we can't keep taking breaks if you want to get this thing done. It's counter-productive. You know that.'

He studied her intently. 'You're hating every minute of this, aren't you?'

Not *every* minute, no. She loved rediscovering her muse, she loved it when their scenes started coming together, she loved staying in Will's beautiful house by the ocean, she'd even loved spending time with Angie and Lily on the beach—and she agreed that, given the chance, she probably could end up good friends with a world-famous actress…

But she couldn't allow herself to enjoy those moments. Not properly. Not when she was living in a fantasy world on borrowed time. One day soon she would have to walk away from Will's life and try to find one of her own. One more fulfilling than the one she'd been living. Because if she'd been happy in the life she had she wouldn't have been so quick to leave it behind, would she?

'Cass?' The thumb stilled, and the impossibly gentle use of her name made her realise she'd dropped her gaze to the beating pulse at the base of his neck.

She looked back up. 'Sorry. Drifted off for a minute. I've got a tendency to do that too.'

'I remember.' He said it with just enough softness in his voice to suggest he remembered it with a degree of affection. Darn it.

When she made another attempt at freeing her hand he let her. So she folded her fingers into her palm and let her arm drop to her side as he leaned back, his expression changing to the unreadable blankness she hated so much,

'It's okay, I've got my answer.' Lifting a glass of juice, he pushed to his feet and turned towards the open door. 'We'd better get back to it then.'

CHAPTER SIX

WITHOUT any idea why she felt compelled to correct his assumption, Cassidy found herself on her feet, matching glass in hand, and following him into the kitchen. 'Wait, Will. You're wrong. You didn't get an answer.'

Turning in the middle of the room, he lifted his chin and looked at her with hooded eyes.

Which left her squirming inwardly as she tried to find the words to explain it to him without giving too much away.

'I' m not… That is it's not that I'm not…' She puffed her cheeks out in exasperation, and avoided his gaze by glancing at random points around the room. 'I guess I just—' A deep breath and a grimace, and then she silently said to heck with it and took a run at it. 'I feel a bit—lost, I suppose. You and me? We're not the same. This living together under the same roof—' One of her hands flailed in the air in front of her body, towards him. 'Well, we're not the *same*…'

'You already said that.'

Cassidy scowled at his calm tone, and the fact that her gaze shifted to meet his and discovered what looked like a glint of amusement only made her feel more stupid than she already did.

She sighed heavily. 'This is your life, Will, not mine. I'm just a visitor here. But this script…it's important…it means a lot. I don't want to mess it up.'

When there was silence it drew her gaze back to him again, then he took a shallow breath and asked, 'Why is it so important?'

Now, there was a question with a loaded answer.

Her hesitation brought him a step closer, his hand reaching out to set his glass on the nearest counter top. 'I get the not wanting to mess up part. Everyone feels that way when they work on a script. Or on any kind of a project that means something to them. There was a time you wanted to succeed in this business as much as I did…'

Cassidy smiled wryly. 'Apparently not *quite* as much as you did…'

The low words were enough to tug on the edges of his mouth. 'Okay. Fair enough. We had different motivations but the same goal—at least I thought we did. Maybe I was wrong about that?'

If she had, she'd have left everything behind to go with him to California. That was what he was intimating, wasn't it? Yes, Will had been driven for different reasons from Cassidy. But the goal *had* been a dream they'd shared. What had broken them apart had been Cassidy's starry-eyed romanticism over the life they would have together weighed against Will's need to be successful enough to prove to all those people who had thought him worthless that they'd been spectacularly wrong in their assessment. Cassidy had believed they would achieve their dreams together. Will had left her behind and done it on his own. But she'd let him go, hadn't she?

Will took another step closer. 'Why is it so important, Cass?'

She took a deep breath, while warily watching to see how close he planned on getting. 'We bombed last time, Will. You remember how bad that felt as well as I do…'

'Oh, sweetheart, I've bombed a few times since then— trust me. It's par for the course out here.'

The use of the drawled 'sweetheart' made her cock a re-criminating brow at him, but she let it slide when she saw the light in his eyes. 'But you're a success, Will. Look around you—this house, your company, the awards you've won— you've made it. I'm a *schoolteacher*. Not that there's anything wrong with that—it's one of the most honourable professions on the planet—but it wasn't something I'd planned on doing for the rest of my life.' Any more than living on her own had been. 'The last script I cowrote with you is the only thing I have on my movie-writing CV. The script for a movie that bombed at the box office and gave movie reviewers globally the excuse to ramp the venom volume up to high—remember? I ended on a failure. A very public failure. I don't want another one. Seriously, I don't think I could take it…and… And I'm babbling again, aren't I?'

'Like a brook.' He smiled indulgently.

Another step forward brought him to within reaching distance. But instead of offering her the kind of comfort-ing hug she desperately needed and dreaded at the same time, he lifted his hands and pushed them deep into the pockets of his jeans—meaning the only way a hug would happen was if *she* reached for *him*.

But that wasn't going to happen, was it? No matter how much she sorely needed to be held—just held—for long enough not to feel as if she had somehow detached herself from her fellow human beings. Now that she thought about it, it was probably the same fear that brought tears of emotion to her eyes when small arms would hug so tightly around her neck on the last day of term…

'It was a success in the long haul, Cass. Or we wouldn't be here. You need to remember that. Sometimes the road to success has its twists and turns. That's all.'

She managed a somewhat shaky smile and a roll of her eyes at her continuing inability to listen to reason or appreciate thoughtfulness without the need to cry. 'I'd just rather skip the hobnailed boots stomping all over my self-confidence this time round, if that's all right with you.'

The green of Will's eyes softened and warmed. 'Welcome to Hollywood.'

Cassidy laughed softly, then stared at him in wonder. 'How do you do it?'

'Thick skin.' He shrugged.

'Is there a store nearby where I can pick one of those up?'

''Fraid not. It's something you acquire over time. Wouldn't suit you, anyway.'

Sighing heavily, she nodded. 'I'd be willing to try it out for a while.'

Whether it was something he saw in her eyes, or something he knew instinctively she needed—as he so often had once upon a time—Will pulled his hands out of his pockets and closed the gap between them. He reached for her with a rumbled, 'Come here, Malone.'

Oh, great. Now she was welling up the way she did with the kids. Only this time it was bittersweet for different reasons. Even as Will drew her close to the wall of his chest and circled her with his arms, she felt the deep-seated sensation of coming home after a long, long time in exile. She hadn't realised how homesick she'd been for him until he was holding her and she had her arms around his lean waist. The scent of clean laundry and pure Will surrounded her, but she breathed it deeper anyway. When one of the large hands on her back gently rubbed to soothe her she had to fight the need to sob uncontrollably. But not just because it was a hug when she so desperately needed a hug. It was because it was *Will*. The Will she'd missed so very much that even while she was being held in his arms the fact she knew it might never happen again was enough to break another corner off her ragged-edged heart.

'You're doing great, Cass. Don't be so hard on yourself. There are days in that room I forget it's been so long since we worked together.'

She *had* been feeling better about her scriptwriting abilities, but hearing him say it meant a lot to her. 'Thank you.'

'You're welcome.' The smile sounded in his voice.

It made her smile too, as she tilted her head back to rest her chin on his shoulder. Then she took another deep breath and forced herself to step away from him. 'I guess I can stand to be cooped up in that room for another few hours if you can.'

'Good.' A devilish smile was backed up by another wink. 'We can talk about Rachel wearing that harem girl outfit again.'

Cassidy laughed. 'No. we can't. She's not doing the Dance of the Seven Veils for Nick...'

'She'd be very sexy doing it.'

'She'd feel like a complete idiot doing it.'

Will retrieved his glass and headed back towards the office. 'Okay, then. We'll play out the scene and see how it goes.'

Cassidy chuckled; he could go right ahead and hold his breath for that one. But she suddenly felt a lot better going back into his office with him. *Much better.*

Ryan and Malone were on top form when they pitched their script for the first time—even if it was technically just a trial run.

Will had driven them into Los Angeles, to his plush, if chaotic offices. making small talk on the journey that Cassidy knew was meant to distract her from her nervousness. It was yet another thoughtful gesture she both needed and feared at the same time. Between his thoughtfulness, his ability to read what she needed—sometimes before she realised it herself—and the amount of mild flirting he'd been doing since the day of their partial truce she was already walking a fine line. If she made the mistake of falling for him again...

Once they were in the conference room with selected members of Will's team, and they began the read-through, something clicked. Maybe it was because she let herself get lost in what they were doing. Maybe it was because, for the guts of an hour, reality was shut out. Maybe it was because they became Nick and Rachel again. Maybe it was the fact their audience laughed and sat forward in their seats with rapt expressions at the right times. Heck, maybe it was a combination of all those things. But whatever it was, it was magical. For the first time since she'd come to California it felt as if the old Will was completely back.

He laughed more, he smiled *that* smile at her when she

blushed as she skirted over any kisses or love scenes in the script, he even danced with her and dipped her the way the script directed—to the obvious amusement of their captive audience. He took her hand so they could both take a bow when that same audience applauded at the end…

Then they spent another hour talking with the team about special effects and storyboarding and locations—and Cassidy forgot she was with a group of complete strangers who worked for Will, and debated with him the way she usually did when they were alone.

After handing out work assignments, Will watched her shake the last hand at the open doorway, then leaned casually against the doorframe. 'Trying to start a revolution inside my production company, Malone?'

'Meaning?'

'You didn't see some of their faces when you debated with me?'

She had—and she might have been worried he was angry about it if she hadn't seen the sparkle of amusement in his eyes. 'I noticed the look on their faces when you conceded anything. I get the impression that doesn't happen too often…'

'It's rare.' He shrugged and cast a glance over the open-plan work area outside the conference room like some ruler surveying his kingdom. 'But not unheard-of.'

'Hmm.' Cassidy leaned against the other side of the frame, pursed her lips and then smiled when he looked at her. 'Might do you good if it happened more often, Ryan. Who knows what creativity you have here, hidden under too many layers of fear to speak up in front of the boss. You should thank me.'

'Or hire you.'

Her jaw dropped. But before she could figure out if he was being serious, he pushed off the door frame and jerked his head. 'Come on. I have something I want you to see while we're here…'

Of all the things she had expected to be shown—fancy office, great views over Los Angeles, other productions he might be working on—a room the size of a large stationery cupboard, filled with piles of paper and sacks of letters pretty much came at the bottom of the list. So when he turned the lights on and closed the door behind them, she turned round and lifted a brow.

'A mailroom? That's what you wanted to show me?' Her voice was flat.

Will blinked lazily at her. 'Pick a letter.'

She was obviously missing something. Frowning, she turned her head and examined the room more closely. Nope—it still looked like a mailroom to her. Not a particularly well-organised one either.

'Pick a letter. Or an e-mail—doesn't matter.' He stepped closer to her. 'Any one you want.'

Okay, she'd play. Glancing at him from the corner of her eye, she made a big deal out of waving her hand in circles before closing her eyes and feeling around for a random selection—not helping with any invisible filing system he might have.

When she opened her eyes and held it up in front of her face, the corners of Will's mouth were tugging upward. 'Read it.'

Dragging her gaze from his, she slipped the letter from the opened envelope and began to read, her eyes widening when she realized what it was. Lifting her chin, she stared at the rest of the papers—then at Will.

The green of his eyes radiated warmth, and his deep voice lowered as he told her, 'Pick another one.'

She did—and got an e-mail that made her throat tighten.

Will's voice was lower and closer when he spoke again. 'Keep going.'

'All of them?' Cassidy lifted her chin and silently cleared her throat, so her voice didn't sound so strangled. 'This whole room is fan mail for our movie?'

'Yes. The studio forwarded it here to begin with, but when it started increasing we changed the address on the website. We get mail from all over the world.' He searched her eyes and smiled. 'They call themselves the Fortune Hunters.'

For the first time in her life Cassidy was at a complete loss for words.

So Will kept going, his gaze locked on hers. 'It started with message boards. Then they launched their own site and it grew from there. There are role-playing games, conspiracy theories—some of them have all the lines memorised so when they have a screening they can join in. They even dress up as the characters at conventions…'

With her emotions threatening to overwhelm her, Cassidy forcibly dragged her gaze from his and reached for another letter. 'What's this one?'

Will held an edge so he could read it. 'California's Fortune Hunters. There are chapters all over the place now, but California was the first. They organise a yearly charity screening of the movie, and let us know when it is so we can send memorabilia to auction on the night.'

'I had no idea.'

'I didn't think you did.' He waited for her to look at him before he told her. 'The movie may have tanked at the box office, Cass, but it's been successful in ways no one could ever have predicted. It's brought people together—it's even been the catalyst for a few weddings. There's a community of amazing people out there who are making a difference to other people's lives with their charitable causes through it. Does that sound like a failure to you?'

Cassidy shook her head.

'No.' Will smiled one of *those* smiles as he reached up and tucked a strand of hair behind her ear. 'If you didn't get enough of a self-confidence boost from the reaction to the pitch we just did, then maybe this will do it.'

She still couldn't speak.

When Will's gaze dropped briefly to her mouth she held her breath, her heart thundering against her breastbone as she waited to see if he was going to kiss her...

But he dropped his hand and stepped back. 'Read through some of them while I make a few calls, if you like. There's a coffee machine down the hall. Then I'll come back and drive us home, so we can work on the changes we agreed in the meeting.'

She nodded. Then watched as he turned round and opened the door. The first tear slipped onto her lower lashes after he'd disappeared. It wasn't just because of what he'd shown her and told her, or the fact he had known how much she'd needed to see it. It was because he'd used the word 'home'.

As if it was *her* home too...

The thing was, somewhere along the way, his house *had* started to feel more like home than the one she had in Ireland. It would take strength to leave and close the door on their relationship for once and for all. She knew she'd be leaving even more of herself behind than he'd taken with him the first time.

They didn't go straight to work on the script revisions when they got back to Will's house. Cassidy couldn't allow herself to think of it as 'home'. She'd already allowed herself to get too comfortable in her surroundings as it was.

Unusually—since she'd arrived anyway—it was raining outside: hot, heavy, humid rain. So they had a take-away Moroccan dinner inside—plates of a half-dozen dishes she'd never tried before spread out on a coffee table in front of them while they sat on one of Will's large sofas.

'I'm curious about your life,' he said.

'Why?'

'I can't ask you a simple question?'

'Maybe I'm *curious* why you need to know.' Cassidy was fully aware of the verbal game of poker they were playing over dessert, but she wasn't backing down.

'I thought we'd decided we're friends again?'

She avoided his gaze, playing with the ice cream in her tub. 'Okay, we're friends.'

'Friends talk about stuff. Try me.'

It took a long while for her to make a decision, and Cassidy couldn't help but smile when he lifted dark brows in challenge. She knew *he* knew the reason she was reluctant to talk about her life was because it involved emotion. She knew *he* knew that *she knew* Will didn't talk about emotion. End of story. He'd rather chew off his own arm. So it was, therefore, a case of what was sauce for the goose…

But this change for the better in their relationship had allowed them to start getting to know each other again, and she was reluctant to put a dampener on that. Especially when they were both smiling more, and working together had got easier, and he'd been so thoughtful of late…

The ice cream took several violent digs before she sighed heavily. 'One hint of anything resembling sympathy, Will Ryan…'

When she glanced up he was continuing to smile his patented humouring smile at her.

She frowned. 'You're doing it already.'

'I'm not.' He pasted a serious expression on his face, folding his arms and jerking his chin at her. 'Go on. I'm listening.'

'I hate this. I tell you about my life and it's just going to sound pathetically ordinary compared to yours.'

'Not necessarily. Most of my life is more ordinary than people might think.'

Cassidy snorted softly in disbelief. 'Like what, for instance? Hanging out with movie stars? Working in the motion picture industry? The fact you attend the Oscars every year? The millionaire's beach house you live in?'

It took a second, then one of *those* smiles broke free, the green in his eyes glittering hypnotically. He shook his head before looking at a point over her left shoulder as he considered his answer. 'It's hard to find words.'

'Will, you work with words every day.' She kept her voice purposefully soft. 'Can't spell them—but you know how to use them…'

'Very funny.'

'Try. One ordinary thing about your life.'

'Just the one and you'll tell me about *your* life.' He looked as if he doubted that.

'Make it a truly mundane one and I'll fill in the blanks.' She lifted her spoon and made a cross in the air above her breasts. 'Cross my heart.'

The move apparently gave him an open invitation to drop his gaze and watch the increased rise and fall of her breasts as he looked at them. Then his thick lashes lifted and he chuckled at her look of accusation before informing her, 'I don't have a housekeeper. So I do all my own cleaning.'

'Oh, no—your obsession with neatness doesn't count.' It was something that had never ceased to astound her, but he'd always seemed to get pleasure from an organised environment. Whereas Cassidy had always lived in the kind of chaos that was reflective of her life in general. In the end she'd put his borderline obsession down to control—the same kind of control that he'd exerted over so many areas of his life.

Only in the bedroom had he ever fully lost that precious self-control. When he'd made love to her she'd never had any doubts about how he felt. But then neither had he about how *she* felt. They'd been stripped naked—emotionally as well as physically. Something Cassidy had never allowed herself to come close to experiencing with anyone else. Not that he would ever know that.

Will shrugged and stole a spoonful of her ice cream. 'Still counts as ordinary. Everyone does housework. It's a universal equaliser.'

Cassidy laughed. 'I've made a valiant effort to avoid it wherever possible, believe me.'

The corners of his mouth quirked. 'I believe you. Now I've lived up to my end of the bargain it's your turn. Tell me about this ordinary life of yours.'

It was on the tip of her tongue to ask again why he wanted to know, but instead she dropped her chin and played some more with the ice cream. 'I teach, so I work according to the school terms. In the summer I usually manage to find work at camps, or at places where working parents can leave their kids while they do their nine to fives. I have a flat. I have teacher friends I meet for lunches or coffees or whatever. I used to have a cat—'

'What happened to it?'

'It must have been about a hundred years old when I got it from the shelter, so it didn't last long.'

'Didn't get another one?'

'Nope.' She smiled wryly at her ice cream. 'Apparently I wasn't ready to deal with another loss after my dad. I cried for weeks over that dumb cat.'

When Will didn't say anything she stole an upward glance at him from underneath a wave of lose hair. He was studying her again. But instead of asking *What?* that way she usually did, she took the opportunity to say, 'Thank you. For the card and the flowers you sent.'

He knew she didn't mean after the cat had died. 'I got your note. You don't have to thank me again.'

Cassidy dampened her lips and took a breath. 'It meant

a lot. I didn't put that in the note. And I should have. That time is kind of a blur to me now.'

'Grief can be like that.' His gaze shifted to her loose hair, and Cassidy wondered if he was thinking of tucking it away again. 'You had a lot to do to wrap everything up as well. At least you had your family to help you.'

'I did.' Unlike the eight-year-old Will, who'd had no one when his mother had passed away; it still killed Cassidy that he'd been left so alone.

'You could have called me if you'd needed anything— you know that.'

She did. Even if he hadn't written it in the card he had sent. 'Wasn't that easy.'

Taking a deep breath, he reached forward for the remote control of his ridiculously large widescreen TV and handed it to her. 'I've decided we're taking the night off. Pick a movie.'

Cassidy blinked in surprise. 'I thought you wanted to get this thing done?'

'It'll wait.' He waved the remote in the air. 'Pick a movie.'

Setting the ice cream tub between her knees, Cassidy took the remote with one hand, leaning forward and resting the back of her other hand against his forehead. 'Are you feeling sick? Do you have a temperature? Maybe you caught my cold…'

He removed her hand. 'You can't spend an evening just sitting doing nothing with me, can you?'

'Yes, I can.' But she could feel her cheeks warming at the 'doing nothing with me' part. Because in the past sitting on a sofa watching a movie with him would have led to kissing. Kissing would have led to touching. Then—

'Prove it. Pick a movie.'

With an arched brow she lifted her chin and curled her legs underneath her, glaring sideways at him as she pointed the remote at the TV. 'You'll regret this.'

Will toed off his shoes and lifted his feet to rest them on the coffee table, settling back into the large cushions. 'No, I'm not.'

'Oh, yes you are.' She smirked as the screen jumped to life and she flicked through the channels to find what she was looking for. There it was. That would do, 'Because it is now officially chick-flick night…'

When the credits played at the end of the movie, Cassidy turned her head against the back of the sofa and found Will fast asleep, his face turned towards her. He was gorgeous. Strands of dark hair falling across his forehead, cheeks flushed with sleep, full lips parted as he breathed deep, even breaths. For a long while she just looked at him, drinking in the sight and memorising every detail. Then she gave in to temptation and brushed a single strand of rich hair off his forehead with her fingertips. Her voice was a whisper, as if she was reluctant to lose the stolen moment. 'Will?'

He didn't react, so she smiled and tried again with a slightly stronger voice. 'Will.'

'Hmm…?'

Still smiling, she watched as he slowly made his way into consciousness. How many times had she watched him waking up? Probably hundreds. Yet apparently, even after so many years, it was still one of her favourite things to do.

Will blinked her into focus with heavy lashes. 'Cass?'

Though obviously still caught between sleeping and

waking, he lifted a hand and gently brushed her hair back from her cheek. *'Cass...'*

Cassidy froze when he leaned towards her. What was he—?

Oh, no—no, no, no, no, *no!* This wasn't happening! Why had he—? What did he think he was—? Was he seriously—? He was *kissing her*! *Unscripted*! No, wait—it was worse than that. He was kissing her, and it was...it was—well, it was...

Oh, wow.

At first she was stunned at how fast her body responded. The heat built like a flashfire in dry scrubland, even though the kiss was soft and sweet and so tender it shredded yet another edge off Cassidy's already ragged heart. It seemed endless, as if the world turned more slowly, while her heart pounded heavily against her breasts. Nothing had *ever* felt as right in her entire life—not one single thing—and knowing that scared her to death. She *could not* fall in love with this man again. Oh, *please*. But what if she'd never fallen *out of love* with him?

Oh. God.

Now she was kissing him back. Stupid, *stupid* girl! What was she doing? It was Will Ryan—the man who broke her heart and changed her life for ever, ruining her for any other man who ever showed the vaguest little interest in her! What was she doing kissing him back? Had she lost her mind?

When the moan formed low in her chest she had the fight of her life to keep it there. She couldn't let the sound out. If she let it out he'd know. He'd know he was making her toes curl. He would know how little it would take to get her horizontal again. Who did that after eight years apart? What was it about him? Was she really so needy that she—?

Oh, it was *good*. She never wanted it to end.

But it had to. *It. Had. To.* So she dragged her mouth from his—then stared at him as she fought to control her breathing, while his eyes opened and his warm breath washed over her flushed cheeks. He stared back. Then frowned and opened his mouth...

CHAPTER SEVEN

SHE couldn't have him say anything. Not when she still felt as if she was drowning in sensation. From somewhere she found the strength to beat him to it.

'You fell asleep.'

Will looked at her as if she had two heads.

'That must have been one hell of a dream I interrupted…' It was the only thing that made any sense to her.

'It was,' he said with a husky-edged voice.

Oh, thank you, god. As much as it hurt, at least it was a way out. 'Thought so.'

Her half-hearted attempt at a smile was met with a narrowed, searching gaze. But before he could say anything else Cassidy pushed to her feet and gathered together their plates. 'I'll clear up down here. You should go and grab more sleep. Maybe you can pick up that dream where you left off?'

There was silence from the sofa as she walked across the room, then; 'What's going on, Cass?'

'I'm clearing up. I already told you that.'

She'd made it all the way into the kitchen, and had set the plates on the drainer, when two large hands settled on her shoulders and turned her around.

'You're the one who avoids housework, remember? So what's going on?' Will moved one hand, the backs of his fingertips tracing along her jawline and pushing into the hair at her nape. Then he unfurled his fingers and curled his palm around her neck—his thumb smoothing against her cheek.

If he kissed her again…

Dampening her lips, and almost moaning out loud when his gaze followed the movement, she lifted her hand to quietly remove his. 'If you kiss me I won't be able to think straight.'

Oh, dear! That tongue of hers just didn't know when to stop, did it?

The brief glow in his eyes told her how much the confession meant to him. But he dropped his arms and then shook his head.

'I know you're scared,' he said, in a low voice that made her stomach cramp.

Cassidy lifted her chin. 'I'm not scared.'

'No?'

'No.' She quirked her brows in warning, and then angled her head and answered his slow smile with one of her own. 'I'm…wary…'

When she purposefully took her time enunciating the word his smile grew. 'Wary is a good word.'

'I have more.'

'I don't doubt that.'

She nodded, letting her gaze examine a thick strand of his dark hair. 'Cautious would be another good one.'

'It would. Even if means the same thing as wary.'

'Forewarned, then…'

'Can't say I'm happy with that one…'

Drawing her lower lip between her teeth, she made the

mistake of glancing at his eyes and found him watching the movement. His gaze rose, locked with hers, and coherent thought left her brain at speed. How did he still *do* that to her?

His next words removed her ability to breathe. 'I'm wary too.'

In the absence of thinking or breathing, she asked him a silent question. And he must have read it in her face, the way he was so very good at, because he nodded, the warmth in his stunning green eyes sending her temperature up a notch.

'I knew what I was doing when I kissed you.'

Cassidy stared at him with wide eyes. He really was so much braver than she was. And because he'd laid it so tenderly on the line for her, she met him halfway, her voice one octave above a whisper as she asked, 'You did?'

'I did. I've been thinking about it ever since the day we rehearsed that scene.'

When he'd kissed her as Nick?

Will took a breath. 'But this was never the part we had a problem with—was it, Cass?'

Swallowing to dampen her dry mouth and take the sandpaper edge off her throat, Cassidy shook her head. 'No. It wasn't.'

Will laid his palms on the counter either side of her body, effectively boxing her in as he took a step closer. 'You kissed me back.'

'I know I did.' She was about thirty seconds away from having a heart attack, judging by her rapid heartbeat and her continued inability to breathe.

'I bet I can make you kiss me again.'

'Probably. But there wouldn't be any point to it—and you know that as well as I do.' She silently prayed he did.

'Why wouldn't there?'

'Because… Well, because it's not as if we're going to end up… Well…*you know*…'

His eyes sparkled dangerously. 'Aren't we? We always did before.'

'Well, we're not this time!' When she wriggled away from him it had the opposite effect she'd been aiming for. Instead it made her all too aware of everywhere his body had touched hers. While she was still catching her breath from that realisation he made his move—he had her hands in his and tugged her forward—then rearranged her hands behind her back so that he had both of them trapped at the wrists in one of his.

'What do you think you're doing?' she gasped.

With a glint in his eyes, and a killer one of *those* smiles, Will leaned her back over the counter. 'I'm not going to kiss you. Don't worry. I'm checking to see how your body feels about me touching you…'

Cassidy gasped, her eyes wide. 'Don't you *dare*—'

As he let his fingers skate across her midriff he watched the reaction in her eyes. 'Tell me you don't want me, Cass.'

'I don't want you.'

'Liar.'

She didn't want him to stop. And now his hand was moving higher…

When she trembled, he studied her eyes again. Then his gaze dropped to the rapid rise and fall of her breasts. But just when Cassidy was about to take the safer option and cave in to kissing him, his thumb moved. An involuntary giggle escaped.

'Ticklish…' He leaned into her, his voice a husky rumble above her ear. 'I remember that…'

'No.' Now her knees were giving out on her.

Will moved his thumb to prove his point, and chuckled above her ear when she squirmed. 'When are you going to learn you can't lie to me, Cass? You never could.'

He was killing her!

'You want me. And I want you.' He pressed a soft kiss to her throat—on the sensitive skin below her ear—before whispering, 'I remember what we were like together. How good we were. How many weekends we spent in bed…'

When he kissed his way to her collarbone Cassidy's head automatically dropped back to make room for him, while she gasped short, sharp breaths of air that tasted of Will's familiar scent.

He lifted his head, placed his cheek against hers and told her, 'But I'm not going to seduce you, Cass. You're going to come to *me*. That way I won't take the blame this time…'

When it fell apart—that was the part he left out. But that was what he meant. Meaning he didn't see it as anything lasting? Meaning this time it would be an affair? Cassidy wasn't sure she could do that. Not with Will.

Releasing her hands, he stepped back and looked down at her wide eyes, studying them each in turn. 'Think it over if you need to. But this isn't going away, Cass. You know that just as well as I do.'

She did. But it didn't make it any easier a decision.

There was an edge of warning to his deep voice when she continued staring at him. 'You need to go upstairs now.'

Or he would kiss her until she made her decision? Was that what he was saying?

'Cass.'

Practically running from the room, she made short work

of the stairs and of walking along the hall—only glancing back down at him when she had her hand on the door to her bedroom. He stood with his back to her, looking out at the reflection of the moon on the rolling ocean, tension radiating from every pore of his large body.

It would be so very easy to give in to how much she wanted him. *Too easy.* But, with a strength that surprised her, she pushed open the door and turned away. Shredding yet another edge off her heart along the way…

He was officially making her crazy. *Again.*

Her disobedient gaze flickered across to look at him for the twenty-eighth time that morning. Like the other twenty-seven times, he looked at her at the same time and smiled knowingly. It was infuriating. And Cassidy was deeply resentful that Will was so in control. She hadn't managed a single night's sleep in three.

She forced her gaze back to her screen and pursed her lips, narrowing her eyes and willing herself to read an entire sentence and get all the way to the end of it knowing what she'd read!

Her peripheral vision caught him moving a second before his chair began to squeak. That was another thing that was making her crazy. 'The *chair.*'

'Hmm?' He looked at her when she looked at him. 'Sorry?'

'Your chair. Don't you have a can of oil somewhere?'

'Oil?' He blinked at her.

Nice try, Mr Butter-Wouldn't-Melt. Her eyes narrowed.

He pushed his chair back and got up. Something else he'd been doing a lot of was leaving the room at regular intervals. But she didn't say anything. She just smiled sweetly when he glanced her way before turning to leave— and could tell from the small, incredibly satisfied frown on his face that he knew she'd been noticing the number of times he'd been wandering off during the day.

He was restless.

Will stopped, turned, and jerked a thumb over his shoulder. 'Thought I'd grab a sandwich. You hungry?'

'At eleven-thirty? Bit early for lunch, don't you think?'

Trying a new tactic, he smiled at her the way he'd taken to doing so much lately. 'I can't go and get something nice to surprise you with either, I suppose…?'

The word '*nice*' made her purse her lips again. If he did one more '*nice*' thing she thought she might scream. His campaign of *nice*—and thoughtful and considerate and caring and sweet and tender—was the worst form of torture she'd ever been subjected to in all her born days. Especially when coupled with his being effortlessly sexy. But, barring brushing her hair back from her face, and smiling *that* smile at her, he hadn't done one single thing to pick up where they'd left off in the kitchen the other day!

When she focused her gaze on his mouth she frowned harder, and felt her foot begin tapping in the air underneath the desk. 'I don't like surprises.'

'No—you don't like surprises you don't already know about. There's a difference. We discussed that many, many times in the past.' He stepped round to her side of the desk and rested one palm flat on the surface, while his other hand grasped the back of her chair and turned her to face him. 'So what do you want me to surprise you with?'

Cassidy's gaze shot upwards and locked with his.

Will smiled *that* smile in reply.

She scowled. 'Stop that.'

'Stop what?'

'*That.*' She felt a bubble of borderline manic laughter work its way up from the base of her throat as she pointed the tip of her pen at his face and made a circle. 'Don't think I don't know what you're doing, Ryan.'

'And what *am* I doing?'

'Trying to wear me down.' Leaning closer, she lowered her voice. 'So that if I say yes to you it'll seem like it's my decision. When in actuality *it's not*—you'll have backed me into a corner.'

'Oh, well, I'll stop, then—obviously.'

'This whole being nice to me thing can stop too. Nice *never* works on me. It just makes me suspicious. You *know that.*' She angled her head and lifted her chin.

Much to her annoyance, when he smiled again, she smiled back at him. How was this tactic *working on her*? In any relationship—including the one she'd been in *with him*—she couldn't remember there ever being the equivalent of a 'mating dance'. She hadn't a clue how it was supposed to work. It had her on tenterhooks. Her damn stomach even got butterflies when she woke up in the morning and knew she was going to see him! Then there was the whole smiling thing she was doing when he wasn't around…

At first she'd told herself every time he left her alone to go and tend to business elsewhere that she was glad of the break. Then she'd been annoyed with herself for noticing every time he was gone for more than five minutes—as if she was so addicted to the sight of him that she missed him when he wasn't within appreciation distance every time she needed a fix!

Which was pathetic—completely, totally and utterly *pathetic*.

When he left the room now she began tapping her pen and her foot again, only stilling when his voice yelled, 'We're getting low on provisions. Want to take a trip to the store with me? Or do you want to stay in there and spend the rest of the afternoon figuring out what dastardly plans I currently have on the go?'

She sighed heavily and tossed her pen down before yelling back, '*Store!*'

They were halfway around the giant supermarket when Will finally did what she'd wanted him to do for days— reached an arm out to hook it round her waist and pull her close so he could press a kiss to her lips.

Rocking forward onto the balls of her feet, Cassidy took a deep breath and looked up at him from beneath heavy lashes. 'What was that for?'

'You were pouting.'

'I was *not* pouting!'

'Kinda cute, actually...'

'Oh, my God.' She leaned back against his arm. 'Kill me now.'

Will chuckled as he released her and reached for avocados. 'See, when you called *me* cute I took it as a compliment...'

'Yes, but my head fits through doors...' When he looked at her she folded her arms. 'A woman ceases to be "cute" the second she leaves puberty and pigtails behind. Don't ever say I have a pretty face either—it means you think I'm fat.'

'I don't think you're fat,' he informed her dryly as he pushed their trolley down the aisle. 'And I don't remember you having this many body issues before.'

Well, *duh*. She'd been twenty pounds lighter before. Not that she hadn't noticed how Will's habit of feeding them little and often and disgustingly healthily had been having a positive effect on the tightness of her waistband, but even so...

Will stopped, waited for her to get to his side, and then asked, 'Is that why you're stalling the inevitable?'

'Excuse me?' Cassidy's eyes widened with disbelief. 'The *inevitable*?'

'Is it?'

'Inevitable? That ego of yours is the size of Europe.'

'That's not what I meant and you know it. It had better not be because of body issues, Cass. I'll be disappointed in you if it is.' He took a step closer that made her take a step back, but all it did was trap her between him and a large display of sweet potatoes. A fact that made his eyes sparkle with amusement. 'Just say the word and I'll show you exactly how far my appreciation for curves can go...'

She gaped at him. 'You're unbelievable.'

He stole another kiss before moving back. 'Takes two to flirt the way we have been of late—remember that.'

I-n-c-r-e-d-i-b-l-e. The man's arrogance knew no bounds. Angrily tossing sweet potatoes into a bag, she lifted a brow at him. 'And this is us flirting now, I suppose?'

'Nope.' He winked at her. 'This is our version of foreplay.'

Cassidy rolled her eyes.

But Will smiled, a hand lifting to brush her hair off her shoulder so he could set his fingertips against her neck—

the neck she immediately arched to the side, to allow him access. Despite her best efforts to fight it, he had a way of making her feel like the most sensual woman on the planet. The darkening of his eyes in reaction to her silent submission was as much an aphrodisiac as the feel of his fingertips on her sensitive skin.

Sliding those fingertips inside the collar of her blouse, he set his thumb against the beating pulse at the base of her neck and leaned his face closer to hers, lowering his voice to a husky rumble. 'Come to a film premiere with me on Friday. It's at the Chinese Theater.'

The words rocked her back on her heels, her eyes widening. 'A film premiere? You and me? Posh clothes, red carpet, movie stars, press photographers—all that stuff?'

He nodded firmly, moving back and releasing his hand to tangle their fingers and tug to get her to walk beside him. 'Yup. All that stuff.'

Oh, no. An affair was one thing—the equivalent of a date turned it into something else completely. Surely he knew that? What she was doing with him was already dangerous enough, never mind knocking her self-confidence again by demonstrating the fact she didn't fit in to the Hollywood set he mixed with.

'I don't have anything to wear.' It was an excuse as old as time itself. But it was the first thing that came to her mind under pressure.

'We can fix that.'

She glanced down at their joined hands and frowned at them. 'I don't think—'

Will stopped and reached past her for brie. 'Good. When you do think you have a tendency to make things more complicated than they need to be. We both know that. It's just another movie night, Cass—this time in a theatre, with fancy clothes.'

Quietly clearing her throat, Cassidy lifted her gaze to meet his. 'Oh, I think you'll find it's a little bit more than—'

'No, it's not. There's nothing to be nervous about.' He smiled almost affectionately at her. 'You'll have fun. Wait and see.'

But it didn't help. 'Will, taking me as your date to the equivalent of a Hollywood "see and be seen" is—well, it's ridiculous.'

'Why is it?'

'Because…' She floundered, giving him a wavering look that silently begged him to let her off the hook. When he stood firm she explained, 'We can't just go out in public…on a date…like normal Hollywood people…'

Will's brows rose. '*Normal* Hollywood people? There's no such thing.'

When he continued staring at her she chewed on her lower lip—and then the babbling began in earnest. 'It'll give the wrong impression. People might think…I mean, it's not like there won't be questions, is there? I know what happens with the pictures taken at these things…they end up beamed around the globe and on the internet and in magazines and… Well, it's not like we're a couple or this is anything permanent. And if anyone knows you they're going to ask who I am, and if they find out we were together before they're going to make assumptions—the *wrong kind* of assumptions. And then—'

'See? Over-thinking and making it more complicated— told you. No one will make assumptions. You're assuming they'll be far more interested in my private life than they actually are. I'm not a movie star—I'm a writer/producer. I'm nowhere near interesting to the press unless I appear somewhere with a movie star. The only time I've ever done that was when she was someone in a movie I'd written and produced. It was publicity for the movie. That's how Hollywood has worked since the golden age.'

'Will—'

The use of his name as a plea for understanding made him let go of her hand and frame her face in large warm palms; his head lowered so he could look deep into her eyes as he told her, 'Quit it, Cass. It's not that big a deal.' Her eyes widened as he angled his head and lowered it even further, his words a whisper over her lips. 'It's just a night out. We're taking this slow and easy…'

It would be so very easy to give in to the heat between them and forget everything else. But if she did then she'd be in exactly the same vulnerable position she'd been before. The very thought of it made her fight for control all over again. Because a very primal part of her DNA structure already knew he was indelibly printed on her body. Nobody else's touch would ever have the same effect on her. She was his, in that sense. Had been from the first time he'd made love to her—when she'd given him something she could never give to another man ever again.

The fact she knew all that held her back. Slow and steady, he'd said. But slow and steady suggested they were working towards something more than an affair. He'd never once mentioned the possibility of her staying once the script was approved by the studio. A brief affair was possibly a way of ending their relationship with the kind of closure they'd plainly never had, and she felt they both deserved that. It was foolish to hope for anything more.

'We'll get you something to wear for Friday night. Angie can take you shopping. She'll love that.'

Cassidy sighed dramatically. 'I'll *think* about it…'

When he tangled their fingers again she took a deep breath and looked sideways at him as they started to walk. 'But it's a maybe. Not a yes. Going shopping isn't an actual guarantee of *finding* something to wear.'

Will chuckled. 'It is if you go shopping with Angie; Eric says she's never once come home with anything remotely resembling an empty car…'

Pursing her lips as she considered the kind of shopping budget Angelique Warden had compared to her own, Cassidy glanced sideways at him again. 'I'm glad we're giving me time to think this over and make up my own mind.'

The sight of Angelique rounding a corner as if on cue made Cassidy frown and attempt to tug her hand free.

Will simply tightened his fingers. 'Hey, Angie—excellent timing for a change. We need your help.'

'You do?' She glanced down at their joined hands, her finely arched brows rising in interest as she looked from one of them to the other.

Cassidy pursed her lips and tugged again. Will smiled and held on.

Angie looked thoroughly amused. 'Am I sensing a problem?'

'No.' Will's smile grew. 'Nothing the United Nations couldn't negotiate.'

Without warning Cassidy gasped and pointed her free

hand at the windows. 'Oh, my God. Is that someone doing something to your car, Will?'

Instantly both her companions swung round to look where she pointed, Will releasing her hand and stepping forward. He frowned. 'Where?'

There was a burst of melodic laughter from behind him. Turning in slow motion, he sighed heavily at her smug expression while Cassidy lifted her chin high, linked her arm with Angie's and stepped light-footed around him. 'I swear. You make it too easy for me sometimes…'

Angie laughed loudly as they rounded a corner. 'He should never have let you go, my friend—you're one in a million.'

Managing a small smile as she set her arm free, Cassidy took a deep breath and plunged into deep water with both feet. 'I need your help finding a dress for a film premiere Friday night. I wouldn't ask if—'

'Oooohhh—is Will taking you?'

'Yes.'

'Like, on a date?'

Cassidy grimaced. 'It's not as simple as that.'

While people stopped in the aisle to surreptitiously photograph Angelique with their cellphones, she took a step back and eyed Cassidy from head to toe, as if oblivious to her fans. 'I feel a make-over coming on. We'll use my usual hairdresser and make-up artist. Then I'll take you to see the hottest designer right now—I've worn enough of his dresses to premieres for him to owe me. Stilettoes for your feet—*naturally*—and we'll need to borrow something sparkly and worth millions from a big-name jeweler, of course…'

'*Oh, no.*' Cassidy's stomach dropped several feet. 'Angie, I didn't mean—'

The most famous eyebrow on the planet arched again. 'Do you want to knock Will on his ear or not?'

Actually, a little return of that particular favour wouldn't go amiss, but... *'Well...'*

'Exactly.' She linked their arms again. 'Rodeo Drive, here we come!'

A cellphone magically appeared, and with the tip of one manicured nail pressed to a single key—assumedly speed dial—appointments were made...

Cassidy was actually starting to feel a sense of optimism. Until they rounded an aisle and found Will talking to a stunning brunette who had her hand on his chest.

Cassidy froze. Will's gaze lifted and found hers. He didn't even flinch.

Then Angie came to her rescue again. 'I'm stealing Cass, Irish boy.'

'When are you planning on bringing her back?' The man seemed oblivious to the fact there was a woman attached to his side. One who *still* had her hand on his chest!

Angie shrugged. 'Whenever.'

Cassidy officially loved Angie—especially when she looked the other woman up and down with obvious disdain before smiling and waggling her fingers. 'Bye-bye, now.'

Turning swiftly on her heel, she leaned her head closer to Cassidy's and stage-whispered, 'You're about to get the make-over of your life.'

CHAPTER EIGHT

TRY as she might to put it to the back of her mind, curiosity was eating her up. Sighing heavily, Cassidy stretched to loosen the tension in her spine. It was her own stupid fault they were sat on the floor, checking the continuity in their rewrites; she was the one who'd insisted they get back to work the second she returned from a marathon of appointments to confirm other appointments. It wasn't as if she could casually grill him about his relationship with a certain touchy brunette, not without him knowing why, so work had seemed like a good idea at the time.

'Hungry?' He didn't look up from the sheet he was reading.

'Getting there…' She leaned over and pulled the sheet she was looking for from a pile. Then her errant tongue worked loose. 'Not all of us popped out for a nice long lunch…'

When his mouth twitched she wanted to kill him. 'We can eat any time you're ready, Cass. I'm easy.'

A burst of laughter escaped her lips. 'You said it.'

Will calmly set his sheet to one side. 'You got something you want to ask me?'

'Me? No-o.' She took a deep breath, inwardly cursing

the fact she *knew* she was about to wade in regardless. 'Why? Have you got something *you* want to tell *me?*'

'If you want to ask me about Diana, then go ahead. It's not like you to be so behind the door about it.'

She shrugged and fiddled with her papers. 'This is different.'

'Different how?'

Darn it—she wasn't answering that! He could whistle.

When she wasn't forthcoming, he pushed. 'Are you jealous?'

'What? No, I'm not jealous.' She scowled at him. 'Whatever you do in your own time is…'

'Yes?' His smile grew.

So she quirked her brows and reached for a sheet of paper she didn't actually need. '*Whatever you do.*'

In the blink of an eye she found her wrist captured by one large hand. She frowned at it and tugged. He held on. She looked up at him and glared in warning. He continued smiling and still held on.

Then his deep voice lowered. 'There's nothing going on with me and Diana. You don't need to worry.'

Worry? She wasn't *worried!* Although it didn't explain why she suddenly felt better.

'Your sex life is nothing to do with me.' Oh, terrific—now she'd mentioned the word sex. Her gaze snapped upwards and crashed into his. And the heat she could see there made her breath catch painfully in her chest.

When his thumb moved against the beating pulse in her wrist she felt her stomach clench, and the need to close her eyes and moan was so strong it almost flattened her. Oh this was bad. This was bad in global proportions.

Frowning even harder, she closed her eyes and tugged on her hand. 'Let go.'

'Cass, look at me.'

She didn't want to look at him. But she forced herself to—and immediately regretted it. 'I'm not jealous. You should be so lucky. Now, give me my hand back.'

'No.'

'What do you mean *no*?'

'I don't want to.'

He smiled the smile that did something all too familiar to her pulse-rate, his thumb brushing back and forth over her wrist in a hypnotic rhythm. She wasn't crossing that invisible line with him.

She shook her head. 'I've made my decision. This isn't going to happen.'

Will continued smiling.

'I'm serious, Will. It's not.'

He blinked lazily, his ridiculously thick lashes still the most fascinating thing in the world to her.

'All right—so maybe, somewhere very deep inside me, there is an eensy-weensy possibility I feel some sort of completely unwanted attraction to you...' His thumb moved down into her palm and started to draw a small circle. Cassidy heard a strangled noise in the base of her own throat. 'But I'm telling you—this is *not* going to happen. Not this time round.'

When his gaze lowered to her mouth she automatically dampened her lips with the tip of her tongue. As if she was preparing herself to be kissed. She saw his throat convulse as he swallowed. She saw his wide chest rise and fall faster than before, as if he was having as much difficulty breathing as she was. Then his gaze rose again, and she felt the force of wanting him slam into her midriff like a punch.

Fighting what she wanted was one thing. Fighting Will's wants was still another. Cassidy knew she wouldn't recover this time round. Not when the image of him with another woman had sat in her stomach like acid for the whole afternoon.

The fear must have shown in her eyes. Because Will let go of her hand. Cassidy immediately drew her arm back to her side, folding her fingers into her palm to hold onto the remnants of his touch while she floundered in a frantic search for words to put them back to where they should be.

When he spoke his voice was rough-edged, and deeper than she remembered it ever sounding before, telling her he was just as affected by what had had happened between them as she was. 'So, how was your shopping trip?'

'I don't think we should go out on Friday night either.'

'You'll find a dress, Cass.'

'It's got nothing to do with finding a dress. We found a dress.' The most beautiful dress she'd ever tried on or probably ever would again, as it happened. But even if the idea of never getting to wear it in public took some of the magic away from seeing herself in it for the first time, she knew she was making the right decision.

'Then what's the problem?'

Sighing heavily, she unfolded her legs so she could get to her feet. 'I'm not going out with you. Things have changed since this afternoon.'

While she swiped her clothes for any dust she might have picked up off the floor, Will lifted his chin to look at her. 'A lot of things have changed.'

Cassidy froze, staring down at him and feeling the same tension between them there had been when he'd held her wrist. She even had to swallow to make her throat work again.

'I know.' There was no avoiding it. They had. But even if they hadn't she couldn't let it change her decision. 'I'm going to put a fresh pot of coffee on…'

She was at the door when his voice sounded again. 'Cass?'

'Mmm-hmm?' She turned.

Will considered her for a long moment before he said, 'Diana has been chasing a part in one of my films for months now. I've never dated her.'

See, now, she didn't actually need to know that. 'If you say so. It's nothing to do with me. I've already said that.'

'Well, now you know.'

She'd turned away again when he added, 'And Cass?'

'What?' She swung round and frowned at him.

'Don't even *think* about cooking in my kitchen. We'll order pizza. Less chance of a fire that way…' He smiled a small smile at her.

Cassidy found herself smiling back. 'Cute. Go back to work, Ryan.'

The third time she made it all the way into the next room, then, 'Cass?'

Shaking her head and rolling her eyes, she spun on her heel and set her hands on the doorframe to lean back into the room. *'What?'*

The smile grew, his eyes sparkling. 'Nothing.'

Cassidy gaped at him, quirked her brows, and then ruined the effect by laughing. She continued laughing all the way into the kitchen, feeling irrationally light-hearted— until it hit her why she felt that way. Cold water was running over the back of her hand when she realised she was staring into nothing as it sank in. Then tears threatened. Spending time with Will was like riding a rollercoaster.

A part of her really wanted to knock him on his ear, the way he did her. And at some point during the afternoon she'd got sucked in to the possibility of being transformed into the kind of woman she wanted to be. The kind of woman a man like Will Ryan could look at and want for more than a fling. A woman he wouldn't want to leave behind. Regardless of her errant tongue, her chaotic life, her lack of cooking skills and her body issues…

Was one night of trying that woman on for size so much to ask for?

The next thing she knew she was back in the doorway, her hands pushed deep into the pockets of her sweat pants as she waited for him to notice she was there. 'About Friday night…'

Will lifted his brows, 'Yes?'

'I'll go, so long as it's understood it's not a date.'

'It's just a night at the movies in fancy clothes…'

Cassidy smiled somewhat half-heartedly. 'Like you said.'

'Exactly like I said…'

He wasn't going to make it easy for her, was he? As much as she wanted her one night, Cassidy didn't think she could bring herself to beg, so she shrugged as if it didn't matter to her one way or the other. 'Well, I have a dress now. So if—'

'I'll meet you in the bar at the Beverly Wilshire at seven.' He looked at her with his unreadable expression back in place. 'For our not-a-date-but-a-movie night.'

'Okay.' She smiled a more genuine smile.

Then he ruined the moment for her, by turning away and

adding, 'It'll be nice for you to get a glimpse of the glamorous side of Hollywood before you go home.'

He'd said it with a complete lack of emotion—confirming what she'd already known. An affair was all he was interested in. She didn't know that man—didn't want to either. The Will Ryan she'd loved would never have asked that of her.

Lifting her chin, she turned away from the door, determination straightening her spine. Come hell or high water she was going to knock him on his ear on Friday night. It would serve him right. Would show him what he was missing.

And then this time *she* would be the one to walk away.

How did Hollywood's elite ever get anything done when it took a full day to get ready for one night on the town?

That was the main question Cassidy had after almost eight hours of preparation. She'd been waxed, moisturised, filed, painted, plucked, tinted, washed, trimmed, highlighted, styled, blowdried, artfully curled, and polished to within an inch of her life. She had been scrutinised by enough critical eyes to make her feel abnormal, and had make-up applied with brushes so soft they'd almost lulled her to sleep. Then she'd had a lesson on how to walk—a skill she'd been fairly certain she'd mastered a few decades earlier—all while being steered away from anything resembling a mirror.

She really didn't think she had the patience for beauty if it took so much work.

By the time she was zipped into the beautiful emerald-green dress that slid against her ultra smooth skin like liquid, she was almost ready for a lie-down. It was only the

butterflies in her stomach preceding Angie's big reveal
that kept her from throwing in the towel in favour of
pyjamas and a large tub of ice cream.

When she came out of the dressing room Angie and her
team of stylists smiled at her like proud parents, while
Cassidy wiped her palms together and fought the need to
fidget. 'Tell me I don't look ridiculous. That's all I ask…'

'Oh, honey—you have no idea how far you are from
ridiculous.'

'Closer to the sublime, actually,' the designer of her
dress added in his thick Italian accent as he beamed at her.

Except in Cassidy's world the two words had a tendency
to go together.

'Can I look now?' she asked, when she couldn't take
it any more.

'After the final finishing touch,' Angie said as she
stepped forward with a flat velvet case. 'Can't walk the
carpet without the bling, darling…'

The 'bling' took her breath away, and her voice was
barely above a squeak when the case was opened. 'I can't
wear that! What if something happens to it?'

'That's what insurance is for. How do you think they
ever sell jewellery this expensive without it regularly being
draped on beautiful women?'

Bless her, but… 'Angie, I'm a realist. If you've managed
to make me look even one step above pretty I'll love you
for the rest of my days…'

'In that case put the jewellery on and prepare to love me
into your next life too.'

With shaking fingers Cassidy carefully withdrew each
strand of diamonds and placed them on her lobes, feeling

the touch of their coolness against her neck as a matching pendant nestled between her breasts and enough money was attached to her wrist to make her feel the weight of every single cent.

'How much is this stuff worth?'

Angie shrugged. 'A little under a million, I believe. It's the teardrop the size of a small fist in your cleavage that's worth the most.'

Cassidy's jaw dropped.

Angie winked. 'Just a shame no one can take advantage of how good it would look on you when you're wearing nothing else…'

Before Cassidy could make a comment on that, her friend stepped back and studied her with a broad smile. 'You ready?'

'No.'

'Close your eyes.'

'You do know you've been watching entirely too many make-over shows…?'

'I never got the attraction of them till now.' She steered her towards a long mirror covered in a white sheet. 'Close your eyes.'

There was the whisper of a sheet the second she did. Then a pause that made her heart thunder loudly in her ears. 'Angie—you're killing me.'

'Open your eyes.'

The woman who walked through the foyer of the Beverly Wilshire was almost unrecognisable in comparison to the one who had passed out on its marble flooring a little less than a month before. Men followed her with their eyes, women looked at her with a mixture of open curiosity and envy—and Cassidy Malone knew they did, because she smiled at every single one of them.

She even laughed at the concierge who had brought her the cold medicine when he did a double-take. Stepping into a fantasy version of herself was an incredible feeling, and one she doubted she would ever forget.

Since she was living a fantasy, it seemed only fair she include her favourite movie in it too. So she headed straight for the tall stools at the bar and made herself comfortable. Then she ordered a martini while she waited for Will, who played his part to perfection by walking in wearing a dark tuxedo that—astonishingly—made him look even more gorgeous than he already did as he turned a slow circle and failed to find her…

With a deep breath, Cassidy turned her stool and waited for their gazes to lock. When they did the expression on his face was one she knew she would never forget as long as she lived. Looking in a mirror was one thing. Being told she was beautiful was another. But it took Will's reaction to make her truly *feel* that way.

With a confident lift of her chin she slid off the stool, walking towards him on heels that made her hips sway with each step so that the material of her floor-length skirt shimmered in the soft lighting.

Will dragged his gaze from hers long enough to sweep down her body and back up again as she approached him and smiled. 'Hi.'

'Hi…'

Cassidy's smile grew. 'Shall we go?'

'Mmm-hmm.' He nodded, but stayed exactly where he was—still staring at her.

'Are you okay?'

'There's a limo at the front door.'

'Okay.' She lifted her carefully shaped brows in amusement and stifled the need to laugh when the move made him frown and wave an arm out to his side in invitation. 'Are you sure you're all right?'

'I'm fine.' But it looked as if he was clenching his jaw as she stepped past him.

It was only when they were in the back of the stretch limousine that he seemed to snap to his senses; his gaze was openly explorative as he studied every soft curl artfully arranged on the crown of her head and brushing against her neck. 'They changed your hair colour.'

'Highlights.'

His gaze dropped to the strand of diamonds hanging from her ear. 'Who gave you the jewellery?'

'It's on loan.' In an uncharacteristic demonstration of self-confidence she turned towards him and lifted her breasts with a small arch of her back. 'The necklace is a doozy. Look.'

The move had the desired effect; his gaze dropped to the deep 'V' at the front of her dress, where the teardrop diamond nestled in the shadow between her breasts. The frown returned, darker than before. Then his gaze shifted sharply upwards.

What felt like his disapproval, combined with her errant tongue and a martini at the bar, brought the words into the open before she could stop them. 'Angie says it's just a shame no one will get to see me wearing it on its own. When I have nothing else on…'

Will sucked in a carefully controlled breath. 'You—

young lady—are playing a very dangerous game with me right now.'

Despite the immediate reaction of her body, Cassidy looked him straight in the eye. 'Am I?'

'Yes. And you know you are.' He leaned in closer and lowered his voice. 'So—unless you're planning on making love in the back of this limo—I suggest you tone it down some.'

Her eyes widened when she realised something. 'You're *angry*.'

'Drop it, Cass.'

'You are, aren't you? Want to tell me *why*?'

'You know me better than that.'

'Not any more I don't.' She studied each of his eyes in turn. 'What have I done?'

'It's not what you've done, Cass.' Will shook his head, looking at her with incredulity. 'It's what Angie let her team do.'

Just like that, the temporary confidence she'd had shattered. Oh, well, it had been nice while it lasted...

Turning her face away, she managed a low, 'I see.'

'Don't do that.' When he tried to reach his long fingers for her chin to turn her face towards him she moved her head back and looked sideways at him, forcing him to swear beneath his breath. 'You don't get it. Whatever paranoid thoughts you're thinking right now, you can forget it.'

The hurt was almost overtaking her. 'Then explain it to me,' she whispered.

Will looked as if the top of his head was ready to explode. Then he leaned forward and hit the intercom button. 'Stop the car.'

'Sir?'

'I said, *stop the car.*'

The second it pulled over to the side he was yanking open the door and practically flinging himself out. Leaving Cassidy with no choice but to scramble, as carefully as she could in her expensive dress, across the soft leather seats until she could swing her legs out and join him—where he was pacing up and down.

He shot her a dark glare as he ran the fingers of one hand through his hair, the jacket of his tuxedo flapping with his movements. 'Get back in the limo. I need a minute.'

'No.' She folded her arms across her breasts, trying to stop herself shaking. 'You're going to talk to me.'

'*No.* I'm going to take a minute, and then we're going to the theatre, or we'll be late.'

'You can go to the theatre if you want. I'm going home.' She lifted her chin another defensive notch as she inadvertently called his house 'home'. 'I'm not going to humiliate myself any further if I'm not dressed appropriately.'

It was a ridiculous claim. Even Cassidy knew that. If Angelique Warden and her team didn't know what they were doing then no one did—and Will knew that too, if his violent expletive was anything to go by.

'It's got nothing to do with how you're dressed!'

'Then what *is it*?' She took a step closer. 'I can't read your mind the way you read mine, Will. I never could. So you'll need to explain this to me.'

'You won't get it. You haven't been here long enough.'

'*Try!*'

Dropping his arms to his sides, he stopped pacing and stood in front of her, studying her for the longest time before he pressed his mouth into a thin line and she got a low, rumbled, 'You look incredibly beautiful, Cass. You know that. And if you didn't you'd sure as hell have known it from the way people were looking at you in the hotel. You're not stupid.'

It was the most back-handed compliment anyone had ever paid her. 'Well, if it's not the way I look, and it's not the way I'm dressed—'

'You didn't *need* highlights in your hair.' He clenched his jaw and continued staring into her eyes. 'Or to be draped in expensive jewels. Don't you *get* that?'

'What?'

Sighing heavily, Will started pacing again, his voice somewhat calmer than before. 'Obviously you don't…but then why would you? There are millions of people in this city who don't.'

After he'd made three more trips past her Cassidy had had enough; unfolding her arms, she reached out a hand to grasp his elbow and stop him in his tracks. When he looked at her she summoned a small smile of encouragement. 'Get *what*? You're not making any sense.'

He shook his head, his voice softer. 'Forget it.'

When he tried to remove her hand, she turned it and tangled her fingers with his, stepping closer. 'No. Talk to me.'

His words were the very last thing she'd expected to hear. 'You're beautiful without any help. You always were.'

'What?'

'Hollywood has no idea of what beauty is. It has nothing to do with highlights and expensive jewels. Those people who helped transform you were trying to put you into a box you'd never fit.' When she tried to free her hand he tight-

ened his fingers around hers. 'You're unique—as indi-
vidual as that giant walnut of a diamond hanging around
your neck—and there was a time you knew that. If you
were trying to remember by allowing those people to turn
you into something you're not, then you're going about it
the wrong way…'

Cassidy took a shaky breath and avoided the intensity
of his gaze as she fought to control the emotions welling
up inside her. When she'd blinked enough times to clear
her vision, swallowed to loosen her vocal cords, and
dampened her lips in preparation, she made another attempt
at freeing her hand and was amazed when he set it free.

Then she looked at him. 'You're right. Partly. But I
didn't let them make me over to fit into a stereotype, Will.
I did it for me.' When her lower lip shook she bit down on
it and lifted her shoulders towards her ears. 'I needed this.
More than I can possibly make you understand. Because
somewhere along the way I *did* forget who I am—and the
kind of woman I always wanted to be. But when I looked
in that mirror less than an hour ago…'

She had to stop and look away when emotion over-
whelmed her again.

'Keep going…'

Shooting a brief frown his way, for the impossibly gentle
tone of his deep voice, she took another shaky breath. 'I was
proud of what I saw, Will. The woman in that mirror looked
like she could do anything she wanted to do—be anyone she
wanted to be. I know you probably think that's silly—'

'I don't think it's silly. I think it's sad you didn't know
that already.' He waited until she looked at him before
asking roughly, 'Did I do that to you, Cass?'

'No.' She smiled a wobbly smile as his face blurred behind tears she didn't want to shed. 'I let it happen to me. That's why I'm the only person who can fix it.'

'Did this fix it?'

'A lot of things are fixing it. Writing again—pitching successfully.' She laughed throatily. 'Debating back and forth with you even helped. I started to remember what it felt like to be *me* again. And I haven't felt that way in a very long time. Then today…looking in that mirror showed me another one of a hundred possibilities. It's why when I leave here I'll leave stronger than I was when I arrived. It's partly why I changed my mind about tonight too—about coming with you, I mean. If I can carry this image off on a red carpet, without falling flat on my face and making a fool of myself the way I have so many times before, then—'

Will reclaimed her hand. 'Come on. We're going to be late.'

'For movie night?'

'Best night of the week, sweetheart.'

Smiling, she let him turn her around and lead her back to the limo. 'Will there be popcorn?'

'If there isn't, I'll find you some. I promise.'

Cassidy had honestly never loved him more than she did in that moment. Not only had he talked to her, he'd listened—and he hadn't psychoanalysed her to death or made her feel foolish; he'd understood. And he'd said just enough to let her know he did.

But then she'd always been a sucker for popcorn too—so long as it was… 'Buttered, not—'

'Not salted.' He smiled one of *those* smiles at her as they got to the open door. 'I remember.'

Standing on her tiptoes, Cassidy placed a light kiss on his cleanshaven cheek, 'Thank you.'

Will looked momentarily confused. 'What for?'

'For the popcorn you're going to get me…'

CHAPTER NINE

IT WAS one of the most memorable nights of her life. Not for the famous foot and handprints outside the Chinese Theater. Not because she managed the red carpet without tripping over. Not because there was a group of California Fortune Hunters in the crowd to support Will's new film, who went crazy when he introduced her to them and demanded photographs and autographs that made her feel like one of the movie stars she was sharing the carpet with. And not just because Will found popcorn, handed her a handkerchief when she needed it at the end of the movie, or stayed by her side watching over her, but allowed her enough independence to stand on her own two feet...

It was no one thing on its own. It was everything.

By the time they were halfway home...no, back to *Will's house*, she mentally corrected herself as she slipped off her shoes and held them in one hand...she felt happier than she had in years.

'Tired?'

Turning her head on the buttery upholstery, she smiled at him. 'I was poked and preened for seven hours—so, yes, I'm tired. But it's a *good* kind of tired.'

'Okay.'

'Your movie was amazing, Will. I loved it.'

Leaning his head back, he turned his face towards her. 'Good.'

Impulsively she lightly punched his upper arm. 'For crying out loud, Ryan. Show a little enthusiasm, would you? The audience loved it too. They all laughed at all the right times, sat on the edge of their seats at the right times... Most of the women in the auditorium were handed a handkerchief at the end...'

'Yeah.' He pursed his lips and nodded firmly. 'You can keep that, by the way.'

'I only blew my nose once. And I did it delicately.' She pouted on purpose.

'The people in the row in front and behind us appreciated that, I'm sure. But the once was one time too many. It's all yours now.'

Now, see—*this* was the Will she'd missed the most. The Will whose eyes sparkled in the dim light; the Will with a loose bow tie and the top button of his shirt undone; the Will whose familiar boyish sexiness was lit up, then gone, then lit up, then gone in the headlights of passing cars...

When he reached for a loose curl and wrapped it around his forefinger Cassidy let her guard down for the first time since she'd arrived. 'Just in case I never get a chance to say it again, I'm proud of you, Will. You made it. You did everything we talked about and more...'

His hand stilled. Then, without answering, he turned his hand over and ran the backs of his fingers over the sensitive skin of her neck, watching the movement with one of his unreadable gazes. When he reached the hollow between her neck and shoulderblade he turned his hand again, tracing the very tips of his fingers towards the edge of her dress.

But when he began tracing that edge downwards… 'What are you doing?' It was a moot question, but she asked it anyway, her low voice thickly threaded with physical awareness.

'You know what I'm doing.' Changing direction, he caught the necklace between his thumb and forefinger and followed it down to the heavy pendant in her cleavage.

The touch of his knuckles against the curve of her breast made her squirm on the seat. 'Will—'

'Schools don't go back for another month.'

The rumble of his voice was seduction itself. But she still knew what he was offering her—even if he was trying a different angle. 'No, they don't. But—'

Cupping the diamond for a moment, he lifted his gaze so she could see the dark pools of his eyes. 'Checking your list of excuses?'

'What list?'

'The one you have to tell you why you can't get involved with me again.' Long fingers flexed away from the diamond and purposefully brushed her skin.

Cassidy felt the impact of it clean to the soles of her feet. 'I don't have a list of excuses.'

'Liar.'

'They're not excuses.'

'Liar.' The hint of a smile she saw on his face filtered through into his voice, and then he moved his fingers again. 'I can feel your heart beating…'

The heart that was causing such an ache in her chest again when he told her, 'Do you know how a lie detector works, Cass? I do. I had to research it for a script one time. It measures a person's breathing rate, their pulse, their blood pressure and perspiration levels. Right now I can read three out of four of those with you. So, while your head may be frantically searching that list for your next excuse, your body tells me something different. But then you never could lie to me, could you?'

No, she couldn't. Not that she'd ever been much of a liar to begin with. But he'd always been able to read her. It was why it had taken so much effort to hold stuff back from him since she'd come to California.

'They're not excuses, Will.' And that wasn't a lie, because they weren't. They were valid reasons. But then she couldn't tell him that either. Because by telling him she would be inviting him to ask what they were.

'Then why is your heart beating so fast?'

Cassidy reached up and closed her fingers around his hand on the pendant, tapping into a little of her newfound confidence as she lifted her chin. 'Stop it.'

When Will angled his head, her breath caught. But he didn't lean in to kiss her—instead he studied her face for the longest time, before coming to a realization. 'You're hiding something from me.'

Her soft laughter sounded nervous even to her own ears. 'Don't be ridiculous. Why would I need to hide something from you?'

He'd already got entirely more information from her than she'd ever planned on giving him. She'd talked about her doubts and fears and insecurities—granted, sometimes he'd guessed some of them, and *then* she'd talked about them, but it was still more than she'd planned. Heck, he'd even got details of how ordinary her life was when compared to his. Though, judging by his earlier reaction to her make-over, Hollywood maybe wasn't his idea of utopia...

'There is something, though.' His deep voice sounded almost hypnotic in the intimacy of the dimly lit limousine.

Working on prising his long fingers away from the pendant proved a mistake on her part, when Will simply released it and captured her hand in his, between her breasts. If he really could feel her heartbeat then he would know it was racing...

Her plea was barely above a whisper. 'Don't ruin tonight for me, Will. *Please.*'

While he weighed it up in his mind his face shadowed. The movement of the limo stopped. When Cass looked through the tinted windows she saw they were home.

She frowned. No, not *home*—they were at *Will's house.* She really needed to stop doing that.

Turning her attention back to the intense man beside her she twisted her wrist and tugged sharply. 'Let me go.'

For a moment she thought she heard the word 'no', but then her door opened and their driver stood back to let her out, leaving Will no choice but to set her hand free. Cassidy bolted for the door on her bare feet—only to sigh with frustration when she got there and remembered who had the key.

As the limo pulled away, briefly catching her in its head-lights, she saw Will's dark silhouette approaching. He took his own sweet time about it too. When he got to the door, instead of opening it he leaned on the frame, turned the key over in his long fingers and studied her beneath the lamp. Just long enough to make her squirm inwardly and feel the most basic of instincts that left her torn between fight or flight.

'Open the door, Will.'

Closing his fingers tighter around the key, he asked again, 'What are you hiding from me?'

'It's almost midnight. I'm tired. And I'm not hiding anything. Key, please.' She held out her palm and waggled her fingers for the key.

'Not till you tell me what it is.'

The calm tone to his voice did nothing to stop the frustration building inside her as she took a measured step closer to him. 'Do I have to come and get the key?'

'You could *try*.' His voice dropped an octave, sending a sharp spark of awareness through her body.

'Don't. Make. Me.'

Folding his arms across his chest, he angled his head a minute amount. 'Yeah. That's an empty threat, isn't it? All talk no action. That's your biggest problem, isn't it? You're afraid to step up to the plate.'

'What?'

'You heard me.' He rocked forward and dropped his chin, fighting hard to keep the smile off his face. 'You talk the talk, Malone. Always did. But the truth is you're a Tootsie Pop.'

Her eyes widened. '*Excuse me*?'

Will nodded. 'Yup. So I'll open the door when you tell me what you're hiding.'

Cassidy laughed, but it had an edge to it that weakened the tone she'd been aiming for. 'You—'

'I'm the most annoying man on the planet, you hate me—yada, yada. Yeah, you've said—several times…' His mouth curled into an almost cruel smile. 'What happened to all that talk back there about being the confident woman you always wanted to be? I happen to know a little about confident women, Cass…'

'Yeah, I'll just bet you do.' When he pretended to search the air above her head for an answer she scowled at him.

'Confident women have the guts to reach out for the things they want. They take chances. They lay it on the line. You used to be that woman, Cass…'

Cassidy's scowl became a frown when he looked at her again. 'Hadn't you heard? I'm now a *Tootsie Pop*.' Whatever a Tootsie Pop is…

'Yes. You are. But not a good one. You have to work too hard at it. You see, a Tootsie Pop is a lollipop that's hard on the outside and soft on the inside—'

'Oh, I get the analogy.' Her gaze lowered, looked pointedly from one of his hands to the other as if she was trying to remember which one he had the key in. 'What I don't get is when you decided bullying me again was the best way to get me to open up. Give me the key, Will.'

He waited for her gaze to rise, controlling his smile before he calmly challenged her. 'Come and get it.'

Her jaw dropped and a strangled squeak of outrage sounded low in her throat.

Will pushed away from the doorframe and took a step forward, his voice lowering. 'Or tell me what it is you're hiding from me.'

She worried her lower lip as she avoided his gaze, taking a deep breath as she aimed for a version of the truth that might get her out of trouble. 'I *am* attracted to you, Will.'

'But?'

'That was a confession, in case you missed it. Score one to you.'

'No, I got it. I'm just wondering what it's leading up to. Because there's more, isn't there?'

She scowled at him again. 'Do you *have* to do that?'

'Do what?'

'Play the *I can read you like a book* card?' She lifted a hand and tucked a curl behind her ear. 'It's incredibly irritating. And you don't know me anywhere near as well as you like to think you do. Not any more.'

'You might be surprised.'

'I don't *want* to be surprised. I *want* to be not standing outside your house.'

Unfolding his arms, he lifted his hand to tuck a matching curl behind her other ear. Her soft intake of breath made his fingers still for a second before he dropped his hand back to his side. 'Whatever it is you're hiding, it's getting in the way.'

Somewhere in the red haze clouding her vision Cassidy had a moment of clarity. 'You're *trying* to pick a fight with me.'

'Am I?'

A second clue slipped into her mind. 'Because everything else has failed.'

'Everything else?'

'This is what you do, isn't it? You deflect.'

Will clenched his teeth, and she could almost see the anger expand inside his chest. His tone was deathly calm. 'Like you are now?'

How could she have been so blind? Cassidy laughed at her own stupidity. 'You've made this all about *me*, haven't you? What is this? Your way of proving you can have me any time you want?'

'You're walking a very thin line now, Cass.'

'Am I?'

To her astonishment he slid the key into the lock, swung the door open and stepped inside. Walking away from her. *Again*. Well, not this time.

Slamming the door behind her, she raised her voice. 'Giving up so easy, Will?'

'Leave it be, Malone. I mean it.'

But she couldn't. She followed him down the hall, continuing to push. It was his own fault, she told herself. He'd pushed and prodded and tried every trick in his seduction handbook to get to her since she'd arrived. He couldn't even be content with the fact she still wanted him—oh, no, he had to push some more. While offering her some quick affair. To do what? Get it out of their systems?

Didn't he know it would cheapen everything they'd had before?

'But then walking away is what you do best, isn't it?'

'If I were you I'd quit now.' The deathly calm tone of his voice told her just how angry he was. And when Will was really angry, he placed it behind an impenetrable wall.

So Cassidy did what she'd always done. She pushed. 'Or what? You'll leave? A tad unlikely, seeing this is your house.'

He turned on his heel so fast she didn't have time to react. The next thing she knew he was striding back towards her, his eyes glinting dangerously as he finally lost control. 'You sent me away!'

'You didn't look back!'

There was sudden silence, both of them breathing hard, the combination of anger and pain palpable in the air between them. Then their mouths were fused together, lips slamming back against their teeth, forcing them to open up and tangle in a battle to take the upper hand. Cassidy didn't know who kissed who first, and she was still so angry she could see red behind her eyelids, but it didn't stop her from throwing her arms around his neck at the same time as he hauled her into his arms and crushed her to him. It wasn't soft or gentle or cautious or exploratory, because passion didn't know any of those things. All it knew was blinding need and desperate wanting and hungry desire and—

With a high-pitched moan of frustration she dragged her mouth from his and shifted her arms to push her palms against his wide chest. He let go. She stepped back. And slapped him.

She'd never slapped anyone before. As he flinched, and her palm stung, her eyes widened with the horror of it. She was opening her mouth to apologise profusely when Will's expression darkened, his mouth twisting wryly.

'*Finally*. Now we're actually getting somewhere.'

Cassidy cocked her head. '*Oh?* Getting me to slap you was part of your great plan too, was it?'

'I didn't *have* a plan! But if slapping me is what it takes for you to let out whatever it is you've been holding back, then *bring it on*!'

Everything in her rebelled against the idea of slapping him again; it had never been an option for her. Instead she grabbed two fistfuls of his tuxedo lapels and hauled him back again, picking up where they'd left off—only this time with duelling tongues. Will turned them, pushed her against the wall. She let go of his tuxedo and started undoing the buttons of his white shirt, reaching for heated skin.

'Slow down…' The words were muffled against her

mouth, and then he groaned and tried again, using his hands to set her back a little. 'Cass. *Wait*.'

Frowning in frustration as he lifted his head, she dropped her chin to focus on freeing the buttons faster while she demanded, '*Why?* This is what you wanted, isn't it?'

'*No.*' Frustration equal to her own sounded in the rumble of his rough voice as one hand landed on hers to still them. 'Not like this.'

'But this is what we do best.' She raised her chin and sought out his mouth again.

He ducked out of the way. 'What is *that* supposed to mean?'

'You said it. It's the one area we never had any problems.' She tugged on her hands in an attempt to free them, while pushing closer into his chest. 'I agree. You win. Congratulations.'

Will looked so stunned it was almost funny. Then he shook his head and his frown returned, impossibly darker than before. 'I *win*?'

'You wanted an affair. We'll have an affair.' She sought his mouth again.

He took a step back and placed her at arm's length; literally. 'I wanted *what*?'

'An affair! That's what all this is about, isn't it?' She frowned back up at him. 'Call it whatever you want to call it. It's purely physical. Nothing more. And, yes—I do remember what we were like together—so, yes—I do know how good it will be. We're both adults, right? And pretty soon I'll be gone again. So—hey—why not take advantage of it while I'm here?'

'You think that's what this is about?' Shaking his head, he

stared at her with a look of incredulity. 'At what point did you *ever* hear me suggest we had some kind of affair? It's *purely physical*? Are you even *listening* to what you're saying?'

When he let go of her and took a step back Cassidy frowned all the harder; the beginning of a major headache was forming at her temples. 'You know I have to go home—what else can it be?'

'I just asked you to stay in the limo—or did you miss that part?'

'You didn't ask me, Will.' She racked her brain to re-member it clearly—just in case she'd misinterpreted it. But she hadn't. 'You don't ask. *You tell.*'

'We're having this whole argument because of semantics?'

Cassidy was rapidly losing the plot with him. Her voice was threaded with what almost sounded like hysteria. 'You've done nothing but bully me since I got here! At what point has *any* of this ever been my decision? A con-tract I signed almost a decade ago brought me here. A script we had to produce has kept me here. Not once—*not once* during the whole time, Will—have I been allowed to so much as choose what time I want to eat! Today was the first time I did something on my own—and look how well *that* went down with you.'

During her tirade she'd looked anywhere but directly at his face, swinging her arms at random points in the air while she fought the need to cry again as she let it all out. When her words were met with silence, she finally looked at him. What she saw stunned her. He looked as if she'd just completely knocked the wind out of him.

Even his voice was flatter than it had ever been before. 'Well. There it is. That'll be what you were hiding from me.'

No. It wasn't what she was hiding from him, darn it! How could he be so incredibly dense?

Taking a short breath, he nodded. 'You should have said something. I could have bought you out of the contract and then you would never have had to go through all that torture, would you?'

Oh, come *on*! What did she have to say to make him understand? It wasn't that it had been torture—well, not all of it. There had been times, yes, but it was the constant battle of trying to resist falling for him again that had been the real problem. Especially when he'd been so very hard to resist! And in actuality it had been a moot point, because—

Wait a minute. *He could have what?*

Pushing his hands into the pockets of his dress trousers, Will looked her in the eyes and told her, 'You're not a prisoner here, Cass. If you didn't want to make the trip you'd only to say so. One line in an e-mail would have done it, and you would never have had to see me again. If you don't want to see the script through to the end then fine; any minor rewrites from here on in shouldn't be that big a deal.'

He'd shut himself off again. The realisation made her throat close over. She didn't want them to end like this. She hadn't wanted them to end the way they had last time either.

'*Will*—' She stepped towards him.

But he stepped out of her reach, the small increase in distance as agonising to her as it had been to watch him walk away from her before. 'You can leave whenever you want. You always could.'

When he walked towards the door Cassidy followed him. 'Where are you going?'

'Out.'

'It's after midnight.'

'New York isn't the only city that never sleeps.' He yanked the door open, then stopped and looked over his shoulder. 'Let me know your flight times and I'll make sure you get to the airport.'

'Don't do this. Not again.'

The low plea was enough to get him to turn round, one hand holding onto the door as he looked her straight in the eye and told her, 'That's just it, Cass. I didn't do it last time either. You've made more choices along the way than you give yourself credit for.'

CHAPTER TEN

WILL had never considered himself a complicated man. He knew what he wanted and how to get it. He had worked long and hard to get where he was, and he had the life he'd always dreamed of—more or less. But then he'd never viewed Hollywood with the same rose-tinted glasses Cass had. She'd been the first person in his life outside of a movie screen to make him believe in magic.

When he'd first met her he'd found it amusing, her Tinkerbell-like enthusiasm for all things cinematic. But over time she'd smoothed off his rough edges and made him believe in things he never would have without her. He'd needed her more than she'd probably ever realised. Having her push him away had been the hardest thing he'd ever had to deal with. So what had possessed him to think it would be okay this time...?

Thing was, she'd only had to be back in his life for a matter of days and he'd known. He'd known he *still* needed her.

Taking a deep breath, he glanced upwards at the cloudless sky. What was he doing? He'd spent the night on an uncomfortable sofa in his office when he had a perfectly good bed at home. *Home.* When was the last time he'd thought of somewhere that way? It was the answer to that question that had brought him looking for her.

But when he found her bags packed in her room he felt his anger rising. *Not this time.* She thought he'd never looked back? Well, she was wrong about that. And he wasn't spending the *next* eight years of his life looking back. This time they were getting it out in the open—whether she liked it or not.

The fact he couldn't find her anywhere in the house or see her on the beach turned his determination to panic. Then he thought of the night before and searched his jacket pocket for his cellphone,

'Angie? Will. Is Cass with you?'

'No. I had my PA pick up the dress and jewellery. Is something wrong?'

Will turned a circle in the living room and tried to think of where she might have gone. 'So you didn't speak to her?'

'No.' There was a brief pause, then, 'You had a fight, didn't you? I swear, Will, if you break that girl's heart—'

What was it with the universe suddenly deciding he was the bad guy? It made Will sigh heavily. 'How long have you known me now, Angie?'

'Five years. Why?'

'I'm the guy you're constantly accusing of never getting involved—remember?'

Another spell of silence, then Angie said, 'Never got over her, did you?'

'Let me know if she calls you.'

With her promise made, he considered going back upstairs to search her bags for her passport. But he wasn't going to go through her things. She wouldn't have flown home without them. So she had to be somewhere. He searched for a note—which was dumb. Because after their angry words why in hell would she leave him a note? It would be nice to think she would have if she'd got on a plane. But hadn't he said to let him know? He was pretty sure he had...

For a man who made his living from words, he apparently had a very poor grasp of them in real life. *Just physical*! Where had she got *that* from? He was going to ask her that. He was going to ask her a lot of things.

After pacing up and down for ten minutes he decided to try the beach again, tossing his jacket over the back of one of the sofas and rolling up the sleeves of the only shirt he'd had as a spare in his office as he slid the glass doors shut behind him and jogged down the wooden stairs onto the sand. Which way? If he was Cass, would he have gone left or right?

He shook his head—yeah, it had always been so easy to get inside that head of hers. If it wasn't for the fact she couldn't lie he would have spent half his life asking dumb questions like *What are you thinking?* But then he'd never had to do that back in the day, because she'd always been so open—something completely alien and fascinating to him at the same time. Discovering she'd got so guarded over the years had been quite a shock to his system.

Looking skywards again, he vowed if he had to fly halfway across the planet to talk to her then so be it. And then he lowered his chin and forgot to breathe. It couldn't be. For a split second he thought he was imagining what he was seeing. He told himself he wanted her to be there so badly that his heart must have somehow convinced his brain to tell his eyes she was there. But would his imagination have conjured up an image of her looking so sad? It never had before. Would he have seen her slumped shoulders or the slight hint of red to her nose that suggested she'd been in the sun for too long? Any time he'd ever pictured her it had been smiling and laughing, the way she had that day on the O'Connell Street Bridge in Dublin, when he'd *had* to kiss her. Not just needed to or wanted to but *had to*.

'*Cass...*' He said her name at the same time as she lifted her chin and saw him. If he'd conjured up the image of her then he didn't care; his feet were already carrying him to her, his voice as calm as he could manage to keep it. 'You're still here.'

Oh, yeah—that's great, Ryan. Let the woman think you want her to go.

He tried again. 'I saw your bags.'

She couldn't look him in the eye. Her shoulders lifted in a brief shrug as she took a shaky breath. 'I don't even know your address to call a cab. How pathetic is that?'

It wasn't pathetic. It was another example of what an inconsiderate oaf he was. Because she was right. He had been pretty controlling of their environment of late. He just hadn't realised it. 'Twenty-one-eighteen Shoreview.'

When she looked sideways at him he frowned. He was still giving her the impression he wanted her to leave, wasn't he?

'I said to call me and I'd make sure you got to the airport.' *Still* giving her the impression he wanted her to leave. He was a genius. He could do better than this. 'Do you want to go home?'

There. That was better. Now he was letting her make her own decision. Then he rethought that, and added a shrug. 'You could stay...'

'It's tempting.' She smiled out at the ocean. 'I've been out here walking for the last hour. It's beautiful. I can understand why you live here.'

Will glanced over at the house that had felt more like a home in the last month than it ever had before, then took a step closer to her and pushed his hands into his pockets so they wouldn't be tempted to reach for her. 'I knew the first time I saw it that it was somewhere you would love. You always had a thing for the sea...'

Long lashes flickered as her gaze travelled up to meet his, silent questions written across the chestnut depths of her eyes. She had amazing eyes: fathomless, soulful, bright with intelligence. They were especially amazing when she was laughing, or trying to hold laughter back. Will remembered how amazing they had looked the first time she'd told him she loved him.

Then she dropped her chin and hid her eyes from him. 'I've been thinking about some of the things you said last night.'

'Yeah. I've been doing some thinking too.' When her lashes lifted he tried a small smile on for size. 'We said a lot.'

She nodded. 'We did.'

'I never meant to make you feel trapped here. I genuinely did think it would make it easier to work on the script. And as for the food thing—you never eat when you're working; it was always me who had to remind you to take a break and eat something. I guess I fell back into old habits.'

Her finely arched brows rose. 'I never thought of it that way. You're right. That *is* the way we used to be when we were working. I still have erratic mealtimes, and I eat way too much junk. I've probably eaten healthier here than I have in years.'

Okay. This was good. So he took another step forward—then faltered when she frowned a little and looked away. Too much?

When she sighed he tried not to look down at the rise and fall of her breasts. He'd never been able to look at her without wanting her. How hadn't she *known* how beautiful she was? He would never understand that. Any more than he would forgive Angie for changing the hair he'd always loved so much. It had been bad enough seeing so much of it cut off since the last time he saw her. When he'd known her before it had been halfway down her back, and sometimes when she was lying on top of him they would kiss surrounded by a cocoon of flower-scented hair. Will wondered how long highlights lasted. Not that there was anything wrong with them *per se*, it was just that he preferred her hair the rich auburn of before. Then he thought about how she might take it if he told her how to have her hair… Okay…might not help him stay out of trouble.

'I guess the fact I'm still here shows how much braver you are than me…'

What? He frowned at her profile. What did *that* mean?

Before he could ask she elaborated. 'I always wondered how you did it. Walked away like that without looking back. I tried to do it this morning, but even if I had known the address to call for a cab I don't know that I could have. Not without clearing the air first.'

It was a 'give with one hand, take away with the other' situation. On the one hand she'd just told him she hadn't been able to leave without seeing him—which made his heart swell in his chest. But on the other she'd basically told him she still blamed him for their break-up, because *he* left. He was pretty sure that was what she meant—in a roundabout way, with a backhanded compliment about him being brave.

Will had something to say about that. 'I don't know what you remember about that day. But if you look back maybe you'll think about everything that went before it. No matter what I tried, you kept pushing me away. You—'

'I know. You're right. I *did* send you away.'

He wasn't expecting that one. It brought him forward another step. A step immediately counteracted by Cass, when she stiffened, turned, and waited for him to accept the silent invitation to walk and talk. So he did.

Waves fizzed against the hot sand, dragging back out to sea to be replaced by the next as Cass pushed her hands into the pockets of her light trousers and watched her bare feet as they walked side by side.

'I always knew one day I would have to take on the care of my parents. That's what happens when people wait till later in life to have a child. And my dad was never the same after Mum died. I just never knew that he would end up sick at the very time we had big decisions to make about *our* lives…'

Will walked silently at her side and let her talk it through. The fact they had time to do it was enough for him. She was still there. That was what mattered most.

Cass took a deep breath and lifted her gaze from her feet to stare down the endless beach. 'We shared the dream of coming out here and being a success. We came at it from different angles, but we knew that. I guess the movie knocked some of the wind out of my sails, but not you. You wouldn't give up. Braver than me.' She smiled briefly at him. 'Like I said.'

'We were supposed to do all this together.'

'I know.' The smile wavered and he saw her look skywards. 'I guess a part of me always took some small comfort from the fact one of us made it. I'm proud of you.'

She had no idea what it meant to hear her say she was proud of him. He wouldn't have cared had it been anyone else. From Cass it meant everything. She was the proud parent, the teacher who'd made a difference, the foster parents who'd got it right with him in his last home, and the first woman who had ever made him feel love all wrapped into one when she said those four simple words. With those words the last remnants of the boy who had never thought he would amount to anything had been laid to rest.

Will swallowed hard and battled with the need to hold her. He had to. But he couldn't. Not yet.

'In the end I had to choose between two people I loved.' She took a shaky breath, 'I knew you would make it without me, Will. I think a part of me always knew that. My dad needed me.'

'*I* needed you.' He'd always thought she'd understood that.

The next shaky breath she took caught on a sob. 'When I sent you away that last time I never thought you would go. I didn't want you to. But I couldn't make that decision for you either. It wouldn't have been fair.'

Just like always, her hurt became *his* hurt, making him frown hard at her profile as a lone tear streaked down her cheek and she rubbed it away. 'You made the decision for me. I would never have left if you hadn't.'

She smiled sadly. 'Maybe I knew that. Everything was

so mixed up. It hurt so badly—every time I look back on that time all I can see is hurt. Maybe it was easier to hate you for leaving than it was to face up to my part in it. I just...I never thought...'

When she stopped, placed her hands on her hips and dropped her head back to take several ragged breaths, Will took his hands out of his pockets in preparation.

'See.' It was half-sob, half self-recriminating laughter. 'This is exactly why I've avoided talking about this for so long. It *still* hurts.'

Will could barely breathe. His chest was too tight. He even had to clear his throat before he could speak. 'What was it you never thought, Cass?'

Sniffing, then swiping at her cheeks, she finally looked him in the eye. And smiled a smile that broke him in two. 'I never thought you would do it. And I've spent all morning trying to figure out if in some twisted way it was a test that I set up for you to fail. But I don't think it was. At least I hope it wasn't. I just never—even when I was sending you away and the words were coming out of my stupid mouth—I never for one second thought you wouldn't so much as look back. Or come back. I don't know what it was I expected you to do. All I know is I waited. I waited for a very long time. Maybe a part of me never stopped waiting. Then, when the e-mail came...'

Tears were streaming down her face as she got to the end and she let them flow, not trying to wipe them away or hide them. Will knew a babbling Cass was a nervous Cass—it was one of the quirks he'd always found the most endearing. But she wasn't babbling this time. She was clear and lucid between catches of breath and the odd break of her voice. So it wasn't babbling. It was her finally telling the secret she'd been hiding from him. All of them.

'I was so very in love with you. I don't even think I knew how much. Not until you were gone. Then it was too late.' She lifted her shoulders again, her voice smaller than before. 'Because you never looked back.'

Will tried to form a coherent sentence in his head before speaking. There was less chance of messing it up that way. He opened his mouth…

'No.' She held up a hand in front of her body. 'Don't say anything. That's not why I'm telling you all this. I'm telling you because we never had closure last time. And I can't do that to either one of us again.'

When he stayed silent she smiled in appreciation and nodded her head, wiping her cheeks dry before dropping her arm to her side and looking back out to sea again. 'I can't stay here and have an affair with you, Will. What we had before means too much to me to taint it with something less. So everything I said and did last night with regard to the whole physical thing— If you could try and forget about it, that would be great.'

'Can I speak now?'

Her gaze shifted to tangle with his, the first hint of amusement sparkling in her expressive eyes. 'You're asking for permission?'

Will pointed out the obvious. 'The "don't say anything" instruction you gave me might have something to do with that. So is it my turn to speak now?'

'Is there going to be sympathy in there anywhere. Because I'm not sure I could take it.'

It was her ability to exasperate, fascinate, amuse and

completely distract him from rational thought in equal measures that had first attracted Will to Cass, so he fell back into habits of old as his way of dealing with it. Reaching for her shoulder, he turned her round to face him, ignoring the fact the sea was washing over his shoes.

'Shut up, Cass. And listen. It's my turn.' When she cocked a brow at him he smiled at her. 'I tried being polite about it, but you took too long giving me permission to speak. All you did was remind me why I never ask for it…'

When he was sure he had her undivided attention, he let go of her shoulders and pushed his hands back into his pockets, frowning a little when her gaze dropped to watch the movement and she looked as if she might be figuring out why he did it.

'This whole I never looked back thing? It's rubbish.'

It brought her gaze back up to find his at speed. 'What?'

'You heard me. I've never stopped looking back. If you hadn't sent me away the way you did I would never have left. Or at the very least I'd have gone ahead of you and waited. All you had to do was say the word. I'd spent my whole life being sent away by people. You knew that. You were the very last person I expected to do it to me—technically I maybe should have been able to deal with it better after so much practice…'

The look on her face floored him.

'But, no, I didn't deal with it better. I don't think I've ever dealt with it.' He lifted his brows in question. 'Do you want to hazard a guess why that might have been?'

Her lower lip trembled. 'Because you loved me the way I loved you.'

Will nodded, his voice soft. 'Because I loved you more than I'd ever loved anyone. I didn't even know what love was until you.'

When more tears slipped free, his hands immediately came out of his pockets to frame her face and brush them away with his thumbs. 'Don't do that. I hate it when you do that. I loved you, Cass—I did. So you tell me how I could feel that much and never look back. No one could. There were dozens of times I tore it apart in my head to see what I could have done differently, but the simple fact was it was already done.'

'I know,' she sobbed.

Stepping in closer, he lowered his head at the same time as he used his thumbs to lift her chin. Then, when he was looking deep into her eyes, he took a deep breath. 'I knew when I sent you that first e-mail there was a chance we'd end up here again.'

'I felt the same way when I opened it.' She smiled tremulously.

'We're different people.'

'We are.'

'But we're the same too—if that makes sense…'

Cass nodded. 'It does.'

'It was when you hid under the pillow,' he told her.

It took a minute. Confusion clouded the bright light in her beautiful eyes until she got it. 'When I had the cold and you wouldn't go away?'

'Yes.' His thumbs brushed across her cheeks as he smiled. 'That's when I knew I was in trouble again.'

'It was?'

'Mmm-hmm. Then I tried every trick in the book to get

you to stop trying to hide from me. Have I ever mentioned you can be really hard work?'

She laughed, and the sound was musical and lighter than before. 'It's okay. I'm well aware of that fact, thank you.'

There was more to say, but it was no good. He had to kiss her. Using his thumbs, he tilted her head back a little more while he closed the last inch between their bodies. Then he searched her eyes, hesitating for a brief moment until she silently willed him not to stop. When he lowered his head she met him halfway. Her felt her hands gripping handfuls of his loose shirt at either side of his waist as his lips moved over hers. There was no doubt about it. This part was right. No arguing with chemistry.

Threading the fingers of one hand into her glorious windswept hair, he moved his other hand from her face, traced down her throat, over her shoulder, and then down her back so he could wrap an arm around her waist to draw her closer. Cassidy moved her hands and wrapped her arms around him to bring him closer still. And even the fact that the curves of her body seemed to fit perfectly into the dips and plains of his had always felt right to Will. Another sign that she was made to be there…

He lifted his head enough to mumble, 'Are you going to slap me again?'

She pulled back a little more and grimaced. 'I'm so sorry I did that.'

'And I shouldn't have lost my temper.'

It made her smile. 'Forget about it. I lose mine every…what?'

Will lifted a brow, his mouth twitching. 'Actually, you've improved with age. It used to be every three, four minutes…'

'Funny guy.'

He wasn't kidding. Chemistry like theirs combined with artistic temperaments and stubborn streaks? Oh, there had been fireworks, all right. But whoever it was who said not to play with fire had sure as hell never had as much fun with it as Will had.

'Now. About this supposed affair I suggested.' It took considerable effort not to chuckle when she grimaced again. 'Are we chalking that one down to the problem you have with over-thinking and letting it drop?'

Cass nodded enthusiastically. 'Please, yes.'

'Good—because that's not what I've been aiming for at all.' He flexed his fingers in her hair, cradling the back of her head and watching the reaction in her eyes. 'I was determined to take it slow with you this time—but to hell with it. I want you to stay. You had me with the pillow, Cass, but you knocked me on my ear last night with that dress. Do you have any idea how many guys were on my hit list before we even left the Beverly Wilshire last night? I'd have taken them on—you know that about me.'

In a heartbeat the Cass he'd fallen in love with a decade before was back, her smile lighting her up from inside. Right there, under unforgiving California sunshine, with her wind-blown hair and barely any make-up, and a slight sunburn on her nose and her lips swollen from his kisses, she had never, *ever* looked more beautiful to him. There wasn't a woman on the planet who was a patch on her, as far as he was concerned.

She lightly smacked his back. 'Now you know how it felt to find you with your complimentary female in the dried goods section of the supermarket.'

'You *were* jealous.' He grinned like a fool. 'I hoped you were.'

'No dastardly plans, huh?'

'Nope. I just want you to stay. I love you, Cass. I loved you before and I love you again. Maybe I never stopped.'

Sliding one arm free, she almost tentatively touched the very tips of her fingers to his cheek. He felt the slight tremor of her touch. The uncertainty was so at odds with the confident woman he knew she had in her that it felt as if she'd wrapped those same fingers around his heart and held it in the palm of her hand.

For most of his life he'd felt as if there was something missing in his life—he'd struggled and fought to find it, piece by tiny piece, each part of the puzzle hard-won but never quite enough to fill the void. For a long time he'd feared he was destined to live his life alone. But, despite how far he'd come and how much he'd learned along the way, he realised there and then that he'd never once felt whole the way he did when he held Cass in his arms.

Her eyes warmed to a darker shade of chestnut, and her voice was sure and even. 'I love you too. I never stopped. So, yes, I want to stay. I'm still here, aren't I?'

Will kissed her fiercely, with all the emotion he'd been holding so carefully in check, and then he held her tight and took a shuddering breath.

'You scared me last night.' He exhaled the rough words into her hair, and felt his heart kick against his ribs when she made a sound that was half-laughter, half-sob against his neck. 'I thought we'd got it wrong again.'

'Me too.'

He kept hold of her and closed his eyes as relief

washed over him. 'We'll get it right this time, Cass. I promise.'

The husky words brought her out of hiding, her head lifting so that when he looked at her he could see deep into her eyes. 'We'll get it right because we'll talk like we're talking now. We don't have to try and hide anything from each other any more. And this is worth fighting for—right?'

'Now who's the bossy one?'

'Right?'

'*Right.*' Will took a step back in water that was up to his ankles, setting her back a little before bending over and scooping her up off the ground. 'Now, we have eight years of making up to do.'

'*In one weekend?*'

'I was thinking more in terms of the rest of our lives…'

0409 Gen Std HB

MILLS & BOON®
Pure reading pleasure™

MAY 2009 HARDBACK TITLES

ROMANCE

The Greek Tycoon's Blackmailed Mistress	Lynne Graham
Ruthless Billionaire, Forbidden Baby	Emma Darcy
Constantine's Defiant Mistress	Sharon Kendrick
The Sheikh's Love-Child	Kate Hewitt
The Boss's Inexperienced Secretary	Helen Brooks
Ruthlessly Bedded, Forcibly Wedded	Abby Green
The Desert King's Bejewelled Bride	Sabrina Philips
Bought: For His Convenience or Pleasure?	Maggie Cox
The Playboy of Pengarroth Hall	Susanne James
The Santorini Marriage Bargain	Margaret Mayo
The Brooding Frenchman's Proposal	Rebecca Winters
His L.A. Cinderella	Trish Wylie
Dating the Rebel Tycoon	Ally Blake
Her Baby Wish	Patricia Thayer
The Sicilian's Bride	Carol Grace
Always the Bridesmaid	Nina Harrington
The Valtieri Marriage Deal	Caroline Anderson
Surgeon Boss, Bachelor Dad	Lucy Clark

HISTORICAL

The Notorious Mr Hurst	Louise Allen
Runaway Lady	Claire Thornton
The Wicked Lord Rasenby	Marguerite Kaye

MEDICAL™

The Rebel and the Baby Doctor	Joanna Neil
The Country Doctor's Daughter	Gill Sanderson
The Greek Doctor's Proposal	Molly Evans
Single Father: Wife and Mother Wanted	Sharon Archer

0409 Gen Std LP

MILLS & BOON®

Pure reading pleasure™

MAY 2009 LARGE PRINT TITLES

ROMANCE

The Billionaire's Bride of Vengeance	Miranda Lee
The Santangeli Marriage	Sara Craven
The Spaniard's Virgin Housekeeper	Diana Hamilton
The Greek Tycoon's Reluctant Bride	Kate Hewitt
Nanny to the Billionaire's Son	Barbara McMahon
Cinderella and the Sheikh	Natasha Oakley
Promoted: Secretary to Bride!	Jennie Adams
The Black Sheep's Proposal	Patricia Thayer

HISTORICAL

The Captain's Forbidden Miss	Margaret McPhee
The Earl and the Hoyden	Mary Nichols
From Governess to Society Bride	Helen Dickson

MEDICAL™

Dr Devereux's Proposal	Margaret McDonagh
Children's Doctor, Meant-to-be Wife	Meredith Webber
Italian Doctor, Sleigh-Bell Bride	Sarah Morgan
Christmas at Willowmere	Abigail Gordon
Dr Romano's Christmas Baby	Amy Andrews
The Desert Surgeon's Secret Son	Olivia Gates

JUNE 2009 HARDBACK TITLES

ROMANCE

The Sicilian's Baby Bargain	Penny Jordan
Mistress: Pregnant by the Spanish Billionaire	Kim Lawrence
Bound by the Marcolini Diamonds	Melanie Milburne
Blackmailed into the Greek Tycoon's Bed	Carol Marinelli
The Ruthless Greek's Virgin Princess	Trish Morey
Veretti's Dark Vengeance	Lucy Gordon
Spanish Magnate, Red-Hot Revenge	Lynn Raye Harris
Argentinian Playboy, Unexpected Love-Child	Chantelle Shaw
The Savakis Mistress	Annie West
Captive in the Millionaire's Castle	Lee Wilkinson
Cattle Baron: Nanny Needed	Margaret Way
Greek Boss, Dream Proposal	Barbara McMahon
Boardroom Baby Surprise	Jackie Braun
Bachelor Dad on Her Doorstep	Michelle Douglas
Hired: Cinderella Chef	Myrna Mackenzie
Miss Maple and the Playboy	Cara Colter
A Special Kind of Family	Marion Lennox
Hot Shot Surgeon, Cinderella Bride	Alison Roberts

HISTORICAL

The Rake's Wicked Proposal	Carole Mortimer
The Transformation of Miss Ashworth	Anne Ashley
Mistress Below Deck	Helen Dickson

MEDICAL™

Emergency: Wife Lost and Found	Carol Marinelli
A Summer Wedding at Willowmere	Abigail Gordon
The Playboy Doctor Claims His Bride	Janice Lynn
Miracle: Twin Babies	Fiona Lowe

0509 Gen Std LP

MILLS & BOON®

Pure reading pleasure™

JUNE 2009 LARGE PRINT TITLES

ROMANCE

The Ruthless Magnate's Virgin Mistress	Lynne Graham
The Greek's Forced Bride	Michelle Reid
The Sheikh's Rebellious Mistress	Sandra Marton
The Prince's Waitress Wife	Sarah Morgan
The Australian's Society Bride	Margaret Way
The Royal Marriage Arrangement	Rebecca Winters
Two Little Miracles	Caroline Anderson
Manhattan Boss, Diamond Proposal	Trish Wylie

HISTORICAL

Marrying the Mistress	Juliet Landon
To Deceive a Duke	Amanda McCabe
Knight of Grace	Sophia James

MEDICAL™

A Mummy for Christmas	Caroline Anderson
A Bride and Child Worth Waiting For	Marion Lennox
One Magical Christmas	Carol Marinelli
The GP's Meant-To-Be Bride	Jennifer Taylor
The Italian Surgeon's Christmas Miracle	Alison Roberts
Children's Doctor, Christmas Bride	Lucy Clark